PRAISE FOR VIVIAN AREND

"Vivian Arend does a wonderful job of building the atmosphere and the other characters in this story so that readers will be sucked into the world and looking forward to the rest of the books in the series."
~ *Library Journal*

"Steamy and sweet complete with a whole host of colourful side characters and enough sub-plots to get your teeth into. A fab read!"
~ *Scorching Book Reviews*

"There's a real chemistry between the characters, laced with humor and snappy dialogue and no shortage of steamy sex scenes to keep things lively. The result is an entertaining, spicy romance."
~ *Publishers Weekly*

Silver Mine is an outstanding story. The author creates a world that invites readers for the ride of their lives."
~ *Coffee Time Romance Reviews*

Arend offers constant action and thrills, and her characters are so captivating and nuanced that readers will have a hard time guessing who the villains really are.
~ *RT Book Reviews*

A full list of Vivian's print titles is available on her website

www.vivianarend.com

A LADY'S HEART

TAKHINI SHIFTERS: BOOK 3

VIVIAN AREND

A Lady's Heart
Copyright © 2017 by Arend Publishing Inc.
ISBN: 9781989507902
Edited by Anne Scott
Cover by Croco Designs
Proofed by Sharon Muha

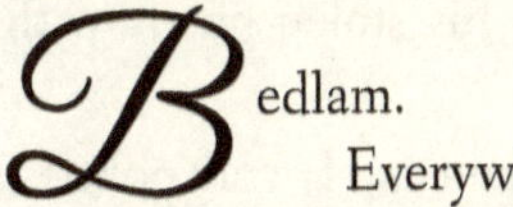edlam.

Everywhere.

Three male wolves chased a couple of laughing females through the common room at the Takhini pack house. Justin Cullinan pulled his feet out of the way in the nick of time to stop from tripping another couple as they argued loudly without looking where they were going.

He swung his paper to the right and continued reading, ignoring the chaos best he could. He'd had a couple of months' experience now, and while he was never going to be completely comfortable immersed in the community-loving wolf shifters, he still found it entertaining enough to put up with.

Loud, boisterous, and in your face. Twitter bio for over half of the members. And the other half, the lone wolves who craved a little more silence, were tucked away into hidey holes around the building. Finding that balance between alone time and the pack they needed as much as they needed air.

Justin reached without thinking and stole a sandwich off a passing plate.

"Hey, man, that's mine," a teenaged wolf complained loudly before noticing who the thief was. "Oh, it's *you*. No prob. You want the rest of it?"

He held the plate forward good-naturedly.

Justin bared his teeth in a grin. "Thanks, this is enough."

The kid glanced around to see who had seen him talking to Justin before he sauntered off cockily, as if he'd done something amazing like bearding a wild bear in his den.

Justin chuckled before enjoying his stolen goods with gusto.

He was still figuring out the nuances of wolf politics. Even with the time he'd been crashing at the pack house, he wasn't sure where he fit into the hierarchy.

The answer should have been *nowhere*, considering wolves had fated mates, mystical pack bonds, and Alpha/Beta leadership teams. Bears had...

Well, in their animal forms they had claws and fangs, and they weren't afraid to use them. But more than that, bear shifters didn't usually willingly gather in groups, or spend a lot of time in each other's company. Not the way these wolves did—

Yet they'd welcomed him into their presence. Probably more to do with circumstances than the fact he was charming.

Although, he *was* charming, if anyone asked.

The past months had seen a turnover in bear-shifter leadership, the political process a dangerous endeavour that had thankfully ended with a positive outcome. A new administration was in place that had removed a threat to all shifterdom and placed his boss Tyler, who was also his best friend, at the helm.

But that was in the past, recent as it was. It was time to focus on the future—not just for the bear clans, but more importantly, for him.

It was good to have a new, more personal goal to pursue.

Justin wiped his hands on a handkerchief as he observed the chaos one more time.

His phone went off, and he hurried to answer. His boss had been impossible to get a hold of for the past couple of days. The man was safe—the security detail Justin had put together ensured that, but heck if Justin didn't miss the bastard.

Of course there were *reasons* he hadn't gone abroad with his friend. *Good* reasons. Good enough to make him temporarily ditch his role as bodyguard to the newly elected leader of the northern bear clans.

"Tyler. You back on North American soil yet?"

The other shifter sighed. "I wish. We were actually in the air when we got an emergency call from the Slovene family."

Justin whistled softly. "Impressive. I didn't expect you to be called in to deal with Russian politics this early in your regime as Bear In Charge Of All Nations."

"BIC for the *north* only, which is a big enough pain in the tuchus in the first place, thank you very much. I guess they decided to hold joint meetings with all heads of state, and in typical shifter fashion, they thought of it one second, set it up the next."

Tyler sounded a little more out of sorts than usual, and Justin attempted to soothe the waters.

"Hey, it's better now than you relaxing at home then

suddenly having to turn around and leave again. What's a couple more days added to your trip?"

"I suppose," Tyler admitted. "Enough about my work. How're you enjoying your vacation from watching my six?"

Someone in the back of the pack house let off a set of firecrackers, the loud explosions echoing with a staccato pulse like a machine gun, and the screaming that ensued was only drowned out by the louder laughter.

"Me? I'm so Zen. The peace and quiet tranquility of life in Whitehorse makes me sad you're not here to experience it as well."

His boss laughed. "You know you don't have to stay with those animals. I can afford to get you a place of your own in town. Heck, *you* can afford to get a place while you're in town—and I did offer for you to stay in my house."

"I'm kind of enjoying the Takhini pack-house experience. It's entertaining."

"Sure it is. And you're not sticking around there for any *other* reason than it's a convenient, central location to deal with work?"

"Pure convenience, you got it." Justin caught himself rising to his feet as the door on the far side of the pack house opened and a vision slipped into the room. "Sweet mercy," he muttered helplessly.

"What's that?"

"*Gah...*"

Justin's tongue tripped over itself as Mandy Ainsworth leaned against the nearest wall and cautiously glanced around the room as if to get her bearings. The petite, dark-haired shifter wore faded jeans that were so pale they'd turned white-blue. They looked soft, as if he could caress a hand over her hip and around her butt, and the silky smoothness would tease his palm. A trim pink blouse with white pearl buttons flared over her breasts, the entire vision enough to set his heart pounding and his mouth watering.

She pressed her hands against the wall as she examined the room, her tongue leaving a layer of moisture shining on her lips visible even from this distance.

Justin suddenly became aware of a knocking sound beside his left ear followed by a high-pitched whistle.

Drat. His phone.

He hurriedly answered. "Sorry about that."

Instead of his boss, a female voice responded. "Are you still drooling over Mandy?"

"Hello, Caroline." He ignored her question. "Are you having a good excursion?"

"You bears are crazy, and don't try and change the topic." His boss's new wife had a lifetime of experience dealing with shifters and all their shifter games, *and* she was far too curious for her own good.

Or his peace of mind.

"Spill the beans," Caroline ordered. "When are you going to make a move on that woman?"

"Considering you're seven thousand kilometers away and fifty thousand meters in the air, perhaps you should defer to my good judgment about the best way for me to go about arranging a date, hmmm?"

"Sorry about that." Tyler was back on the line. "I tried to explain to Caro that you don't need any help with your love life—"

"—he hasn't convinced me yet," she shouted in the background.

Justin laughed even as he kept an eye on Mandy who was slowly inching toward the kitchen. "I'll answer both your questions, because I know you've got me on speakerphone. You know *exactly* why I'm stationed in

Whitehorse. No, Caroline, I don't need any help with my love life. Yes, Tyler, I have everything else under control, with both the diamond factory and Harrison Enterprises, even though I *am* slightly distracted by...*something else*. I've had enough years of multitasking, though. I'm fairly certain I can handle the situation. Are we clear?"

Caroline made a huffing sound.

Tyler chuckled. "I told you, sweetheart. Now say goodbye to Justin so I can give him some final work instructions."

"Goodbye, Justin. I expect a wedding invitation—no eloping, you got it?"

"Goodbye, Caroline."

Background noises quieted as Tyler put the phone back to regular mode before he spoke. "She really does care about you," he offered in apology.

"Caroline's lived her entire life around wolves—if she wasn't trying to interfere I'd be worried something was wrong."

"But you're doing okay?" Tyler asked sincerely.

Mandy fully lifted her gaze off the floor for the first time since she'd entered the room. When she spotted Justin looking in her direction, her eyes went wide and she stumbled for a second before offering a small smile.

"I'm doing wonderfully," Justin said. "Let me know if any emergencies arise, but otherwise, trust me. I've got the business side of things under control, and I'm working on the *other* parts."

"I know you are. Have fun with that," his boss and friend said with a soft laugh. "The *other parts* are worth the trouble. Most of the time."

"I heard that," Caroline said in the background.

"Of course you did," Tyler told her. "Excuse me, Justin. I have a wife to deal with..."

Her shriek of laughter cut off into dead air as Tyler hung up, probably with his woman draped over his shoulder en route to the private plane's bedroom.

Justin tucked his phone into his pocket then straightened his tie, smoothing it over his shirt as he wove his way through the laughing-talking-fighting collection of shifters milling around the living room.

He was a bear in a wolf den—and the real reason he'd remained in town stood mere meters away. Even a few weeks ago she'd tried to avoid him altogether, but today she offered a shy, yet welcoming smile that sent a thrill through him from top to bottom.

While his bear would've enjoyed more luxurious and mellow accommodations, if living in werewolf central was what he had to deal with to get close to the woman of his dreams?

Bring on the chaos—Justin was ready to face *anything* for her.

Lady Mandy Ainsworth ordered her heart to slow down. It was pumping hard enough to power a high-speed motorboat, but all the willpower in the world only eased the edges of her adrenaline-fed reaction.

Adrenaline? Yes, but from good causes, not bad.

She was still in the crowded Takhini pack house, a guest in the wolves' home...but the one place where it was most important, something had changed.

It was that small yet vital change that gave her the strength to meet the big, sexy grizzly shifter in the eye. Surrounded by a sea of motion, the energetic and happy wolves of the combined Whitehorse packs flowed past, oblivious to how rapidly her world had tilted with the arrival of word from her lawyer.

She wasn't scared of Justin. As broad and as tall and as handsome as he was, she'd seen the way he looked at her before carefully turning his back and giving her space.

And it was a fine back, all six foot six of it, covered with sturdy muscles and most usually a devilishly expensive suit. As the assistant and bodyguard to a very rich man, Justin dressed and acted far more like his boss's colleague than his flunky.

She appreciated how he looked in the suit, but she enjoyed his more casual look as well. The soft flannel shirt he'd worn the previous day layered over a dark T-shirt had made her fingers itch to touch.

To stroke, and pet...

...and there went her heart rate again. Because while the thought of becoming intimate with the big beast might make her animal side sit up and preen, it also carried her into dangerous territory.

She'd been the possession of a wealthy man before, and that situation never ended well for the possessions.

No. That direction lies madness.

Mandy was working hard to make sure her previous relationship didn't define her forever, but she was not about to throw away the lesson she'd been forced to learn. Protecting herself—body and soul—was not wrong. This next bit of time was for her, and she was determined to make the most of it.

Big sexy bears would just have to fit themselves into her agenda.

Someone leaned against the wall by Mandy's side,

folding their arms and staring into the room while standing quiet guard. The female Alpha of the wolf pack, Amy, waved back to someone in the gathering, but mostly she just stood there like a sentinel, waiting for Mandy to speak.

"You don't have to protect me, you know. I trust your people," Mandy shared.

Amy shrugged. "Don't consider it protection. Just a friend looking out for a friend." She twisted to face her. "How are you doing this fine evening? And who are you thinking of, as if I couldn't already scent it?"

Her cheeks must've gone instantly red, and Mandy looked back across the room to discover Justin had been interrupted by the male half of the Takhini leadership team. Evan stood with his arms folded, his body a solid roadblock between the debonair bear and where she and Amy were chatting. Justin was clearly attempting in vain to cut the conversation short.

Mandy's embarrassment turned to amusement. "You wolves really have a problem with privacy," she complained.

Her friend offered a grin. "I'm glad you're ready to move out of the pack house." She held up a hand. "To be clear, we would never kick you out, but for the sake of our youth's delicate sensitivities it's great that you're moving your *courtship* to a more private location."

Oh My Word. Mandy's jaw hit the floor then bounced back into position. "That's rushing things a little. *Courtship?* I'm moving out and yes, I'm ready to move on, but I'm not getting myself tangled into another relationship right away."

"Oh, honey, don't lie to yourself. You and me both know you've had your eye on the big sexy brute since day one of getting yourself free from that rat bastard you used to call a husband—and the offer's still open, by the way, if you ever want me to rip out Todd's throat."

"That won't be necessary," Mandy insisted. Her marriage to Todd Ainsworth had been an arranged event, complicated by family secrets that had sealed her lips. It was only a couple months earlier that his cruelty and lust for power had come to light and allowed her to escape. "The last I heard, he's broke and being made to work to provide restitution to the people he hurt. I'd like him to stay alive so he has to toil for as long as possible."

Amy patted her on the arm. "You're far less bloodthirsty than me, but your choice." She reached into her back pocket and pulled out a room card. "This is for you."

Mandy accepted the plastic rectangle, looking it over carefully. "Keys to the kingdom?"

"Suite at the top of the Goldenside Manor. A little more privacy than the single room where you've been camping out, and a lot nicer than the hotel room you booked. Spectacular view of the Yukon River from the living room and master suite. It's yours for as long as you like."

Mandy gave the Alpha a heartfelt squeeze. "You've been so generous. I feel as if I haven't done anything except take advantage of you."

"At some point you'll pay that favour forward," Amy assured her. "Maybe not to me, but to someone else. That counts."

"I'll be sure to do that."

Amy cleared her throat. "By the way, I already had your bags moved to the suite. Oops?"

Mandy laughed. "You're bossy."

"Guilty, but I mean well."

A flutter of excitement tickled Mandy's belly. It was

time to make the next move. "Does Evan plan to keep Justin standing in the middle of the room for the entire evening?"

"If you want him to." Amy offered a sly smile. "It's good to see you ready to move on."

Mandy straightened up, nodding her agreement. "It's good to feel ready to move on, and in fact, there's something I need to do before I leave. Excuse me?"

With a broad arm sweep, Amy gestured her to the center of the living space before responding to someone's call from the kitchen.

Mandy watched her friend leave the room, then gathered her courage and forced herself to leave the safety of the wall. Her feet refused to move quickly, but then again she reassured herself, it didn't matter if she did this in an all-out run as long as she did it.

Crossing the room took mere seconds, and she boldly stepped between the men.

Justin jerked back in surprise.

The Takhini Alpha turned to her with a broad grin. "Lady Mandy. So happy to see you this evening."

Evan took her by the hand and pressed his lips to her knuckles.

Every wolf in the room froze, and the sudden hush made Justin's deep growl echo all the louder.

Evan rolled his eyes, dropping her hand to smack his fists to his hips as he pivoted on one heel, glaring around the room. "Good grief, do none of you have even the *slightest* understanding of chivalry? I wasn't *kissing* kissing her, you fools."

Some card in the back shouted what they were all thinking. "If Amy spots you *not kissing kissing* anyone again, she's gonna rip off your lips. That'd make it really hard to *not kiss kiss*, period."

"*Hardy har har*," Evan muttered, before shaking his head sadly as he turned back to Mandy. "So much for trying to impress you."

She caught his fingers in hers and gave them a squeeze. "All your wolves have impressed me. Thank you for your hospitality these past months, and for your kindness to me."

He'd been the next best thing to a father figure for the past while, and now he looked her over carefully, caring in his expression. "Sounds as if you're ready to say goodbye."

Beside her, Justin tensed as if nervous to hear her response.

"It's time for me to move on, but I'm not going far. At least, not at first. I have some decisions to make."

"We'll always have a place for you," Evan promised. His gaze darted back and forth between her and the bear before a devilish smile lit his face. "Here, I'll get Shaun to drive you. Or better yet…"

He gave a low whistle.

Instantly a handsome, dark-skinned wolf popped up at his side, grin in place as the young man glanced in quick appreciation over Mandy before averting his eyes. "Yo, Alpha-dude. What's hanging?"

Evan pinched the bridge of his nose. "Kent, do you remember our discussion about showing a little more respect?"

"What's…*happening?*"

"Better."

Evan offered an apologetic smile. "Have you met Kent yet? He's Caroline's younger brother. He's supposed to be learning to be my assistant, but he's mostly a pain in the ass."

"Younger siblings have that gift," Mandy suggested, but she smiled at the young man.

"Kent, drive our friend where she needs to go for the night. You'll probably want to pick up some groceries and—"

"I'll take care of Mandy," Justin interrupted, loud and clear.

He'd stepped closer, one foot between her and the new wolf. Everything about the way Justin held himself made it clear he was staking a claim, and that flutter of anticipation inside her belly raced in a new and unexpected direction.

She twisted on the spot and looked up.

And up.

And up a bit more.

Jeez, he was big.

Mandy swallowed her fears and forced every bit of authority possible into her voice. "Excuse me? Did I *ask* you to take care of me?"

A whole lot of *oh shit, what did I just do?* hit his expression, and Justin backpedaled rapidly. "Um, no, but I thought that—"

Mandy slapped up a hand to gesture for him to stop.

She liked him, she really did, but if this was going to work, he had to figure this out now, and not a moment later. "And did *you* ask if you could take care of me?"

He, and the entire room of wolves—who were watching breathlessly as if this was the best live soap opera ever—all shook their heads. It was like being surrounded by a room of bobbleheads, and she bit her lip so she didn't burst out laughing and ruin everything.

Instead, she drew herself up as regally as possible. "Then, I'd suggest you try again—some other time. Tonight *Kent* is taking me to my new home."

She turned on her heel and walked away without looking back.

2

———

ustin stared at the solid wood door as it swung closed behind her.

Something inside him went dark, and he damn near bit his tongue in two to keep from letting loose a roar of frustration.

The simultaneous desires hit. He needed to a) chase after Mandy and b) put the young pup Kent into a shallow grave.

The only thing that kept him from bolting for the door to complete both tasks was the iron grip Evan had on his elbow. Justin could break the hold, but he'd probably break most of the pack house at the same time.

Instead he waited until the entire room exploded back to high-volume. The instant Evan's hold loosened, Justin was outside so fast the relative quiet made his ears ring.

He was in time to see one of the pack cars pull out from the parking lot behind the house. Kent wiggled his fingers tauntingly before turning into the traffic and heading east.

Justin looked forward to dismembering the bastard. Slowly, one piece at a time. Possibly with his bare hands.

It was cool outside, edging toward freezing, although snow hadn't yet arrived, but he was more than warm enough. Not only his shifter blood, but anger and frustration gave him the ability to ignore the weather and march double-quick after the car.

Unfortunately, he had to slow his furious pace to get past a group of young people, and by the time he'd reached the main street, the vehicle was nowhere in sight.

Continue to track her, or use his resources?

Both. He hauled out his phone and hit the number for the Takhini Alpha even as he kept walking toward downtown.

Evan answered with laughter in his voice. "I have to say, that was pretty impressive. I didn't realize you bears could move that quickly."

The man had spoken teasingly, but Justin wasn't in the mood. "Where's he taking her?" he demanded.

At the other end of the line, the head honcho for the wolves clicked his tongue in disapproval as if speaking to a two-year-old. "Really? Of all people, I never thought I'd have to give *you* lessons in diplomacy. That's what you're going to open with? In that tone of voice?"

"Don't mistake the fact I've been polite for two months to mean I'm weak," Justin snapped. "Tell me where the hell you've hidden her or else."

Even as he spoke he realized he should have held his tongue, but it was too late. The speaker on his phone shrieked as a full-out roar of chastisement was followed by more animalistic babbling.

Dammit. Wolves were so freaking emotional. Justin waited impatiently for Evan to stop swearing in wolf.

It took a while.

When he finally did calm down enough to speak, Evan

was still pretty growly. "I'm going to pretend you didn't just say that. I'm going to pretend that you're feeling a little testy because the woman you've been mooning over ever since I met you just slapped your fingers away from the cookie jar. And because I understand what kind of hell that can do to a man, I'm going to be magnanimous and erase your last comments from my memory before we start a war over a woman who made it very clear what she wanted."

Justin pulled to a stop outside one of the closed shops, forcing himself to get his own temper under control. The last thing he wanted to cause was an inter-species incident.

To top it off, the bastard was right.

Didn't mean Justin had to like it. "Message received," he said grudgingly.

"Good evening, my fine ursine friend. What can I do for you?" Evan might have as fine a hair-trigger as Justin, but his sense of humour was definitely more wolf than bear. Quick to anger, quick to move on. "Oh, and I think I'm going to call you Flash from now on," Evan informed him.

Peachy keen. A nickname from the wolves. He was never going to live that down.

Justin forced ultimate politeness into his question. "I was wondering if you knew where Mandy might have gone tonight?"

"Yes."

Justin waited.

Silence on the other end.

Bastard. "Would you mind *telling* me where Mandy has gone for the evening?" Justin enunciated each word as if he were about to choke on them.

"...no, I don't think I can do that. Talk to you later, Flash."

The connection went dead, and Justin stepped into

the nearest alleyway to finally let his roar of frustration escape, the bearlike sounds ripping from his human throat and leaving it raw, which matched the sensation inside him.

He punched in Amy's number.

"You are one brave son of a bitch," Amy announced in greeting. "Last time I saw Evan that mad, someone ended up dead."

"Pissing your mate off was never my intention."

"I'd hate to see what would happen if you tried to be annoying. Honestly, save your breath. I already know what you're going to ask, and if you make one wrong move, I'll warn you now Evan is the least of your worries."

Justin leaned an arm against the nearest brick wall and counted to ten so he could respond softly. "I'll remind you she's not one of your pack."

"And I'll remind you there's pack, there's family and there's friends. I consider Mandy all three, so you watch your p's and q's, buster. I've always wanted a bearskin rug in front of my fireplace."

She cut the call short and left him with dead air.

Justin spent a few minutes cursing creatively before the small voice in his head that had been trying to get his attention the entire time finally wiggled past all the testosterone.

Why not call Mandy?

Flipping genius.

He took a quick walk around the block first, to practice saying *hello*. He got some strange looks from people who scurried out of his way, but it wasn't his fault he towered over most of them by nearly a foot. Their wide-eyed retreats helped him realize snapping, growling or otherwise greeting Mandy any way other than with the iron grip of control he'd maintained for the past two months would only get him in more trouble.

Evan didn't really scare him.

Amy? He was a smart enough man to fear womanly wrath.

But Mandy hanging up on him would gut him.

He sat on a park bench, crossed his fingers and made the call.

"Hello?" Pure innocence and just a hint of curiosity in her tone.

Only...Mandy had call display. Justin had installed it on her phone himself so she'd never have to worry about her ex-husband trying to get in touch. She knew it was him, but if she wanted to play the game this way, he'd play along.

"Good evening, Mandy. I hope Kent got you settled for the evening." He wished nothing of the kind. Even thinking of the young pup near her made him grind his teeth hard enough his jaw ached.

"I'm quite comfortable, thank you. And you?" she asked. "I hope I wasn't too rude earlier."

"You know I was the one out of line," he admitted. "I'm sorry."

"Thank you."

Then she waited in silence until he remembered he'd been the one to call her. "I was wondering if you'd like some company."

Say yes. Say yes. Say yes.

"I think I'll settle in for the night." She dashed his hopes before offering a breadcrumb. "Would you like to get together for breakfast? I was thinking about tea and muffins at Midnight Sun around eight o'clock, if you're interested—"

"Yes," he got out before she could even finish issuing the invitation. "I'd like that very much."

"Then I'll see you there?"

"With bells on," he promised.

Soft laughter drifted over the line. "That won't be necessary. Just casual. Two friends meeting to start their day."

They said goodbye, but the whole time the *two friends* business kept ringing through his brain.

Friends? Not bloody likely. Maybe that's where he'd have to start, but that was *not* where they were going to finish.

MANDY PULLED on a light jacket and left the apartment, taking the stairs instead of the elevator. The coffee shop wasn't very far away, and she needed to burn off a little energy before facing the big bruin who could make her legs quiver and turn her insides to jelly with a single lazy smile.

The sidewalk was firm underfoot, and she strode easily toward her destination, pleased she'd completed her first night of true independence.

No, scratch that—

She was still living at the convenience of the wolf pack while waiting for her financial information to come through. Once it did, she intended to pay them back for everything, not because they expected it but because it was an important step for her in truly becoming her own woman again.

The woman who'd gotten lost when she'd married Todd Ainsworth.

Eight years she'd been with the man. Eight years of her life that she'd never get back. She wished it had been possible to leave him earlier, but she couldn't dwell on that now. She was looking forward, not back.

Last night before going to bed she'd sent an email to her family. The first one in over eight years—for good reason—and she was already anticipating their answer with hope and dread.

So many decisions loomed, but for now, until she heard from them, she was going to move ahead with her plans.

The warm air and delicious smells of the coffee shop greeted her like a friendly hug as she walked through the door, stepping to one side automatically with her back against the wall as she took a first cautious look around.

Some lessons had dug in deep. But perhaps it wasn't a bad thing to be alert and vigilant.

A familiar couple waved at her from a nearby table, and she made her way over to greet them. "If you keep doing this, I'll think you're following me," she warned the wolf Alphas.

"Total coincidence," Amy insisted.

"We're just flies on the wall," Evan countered.

Mandy laughed. "I've heard of horse flies and sand flies, but now you've got me curious to see what a wolf fly looks like."

Evan grinned. "Handsome buggers, I hear."

She spoke with them for a moment before going to the counter and ordering two coffees and an assortment of breakfast items. They promised to deliver the food, so she went and nabbed an empty table by the window, somewhat surprised Justin wasn't already there.

The food arrived the same time he did. He pulled out the tiny chair and attempted to wiggle his bulk into the limited space.

The person seated behind him grew wide-eyed and

panicked for a moment, and Mandy gave herself a mental slap. "I forgot how much room you take."

She shuffled her chair back and tugged the table closer.

Justin tucked his elbows in a little tighter and offered a smile. Picking up the coffee cup in front of him, he held it out in a toast. "Good morning."

"Good morning."

They clinked cups then drank deeply. The entire time his gaze drifted between her and the others in the shop as if he were on surveillance, determined to keep her safe.

He gestured toward the wolves. "Were the babysitters your idea? Not that there's anything wrong with that," he hurried on, "Just wondering."

"Complete coincidence," Mandy told him. "Like wolf flies on the wall."

Evan and Amy snickered from their position across the room, and both she and Justin twisted toward the wolves before turning back to face each other.

"Damn snoopy buggers," Justin whispered. "That bionic wolf hearing is going to get them in trouble someday."

Right— She'd forgotten that detail. It didn't matter that they were sitting far away, Amy and Evan could hear every word as if she were speaking through a megaphone.

"Maybe it wasn't such a good idea to meet in public," she began before reconsidering.

The wolves were her friends, and they were only looking out for her. And if she truly was taking control of her life that meant not worrying about what others thought of her plans.

"Ignore them," Mandy ordered. "I've got some good news to share."

Justin turned his attention on her as if she were the only one in the room. "Good news is always good."

Mandy nodded. "My divorce papers came."

His eyes widened in approval. "Well, congratulations."

"I've been waiting for them to go through. I know according to shifter law he's been out of my life for a while, but I wanted to make sure there were no further legal entanglements."

Because the one thing she could trust Ainsworth to do was mess up her life any way he could, the vindictive bastard. Not just her life, but her family's.

Justin's fingers twitched on the table where they lay only inches from hers. "I'm pleased for you. So...what does this mean? What are your plans?"

She kept her gaze fixed on the coffee cup to avoid letting him read her thoughts. "Plans?"

"Are you moving? Getting a job?"

He seemed to have a whole lot of other unasked questions hovering on the tip of his tongue. The control he showed leaving them unasked impressed her. "I have no plans on getting a job immediately, but I have put some things in motion for down the road." Her email to family. "In the meantime, I've made a list."

"Hmm." He examined her face. "A bucket list?"

"Not as big and shiny as that. It's probably silly, but there are a lot of ordinary things I've never gotten a chance to try." She smiled at him. "I think you know that I grew up in fairly fancy circumstances."

"*Lady* Amanda." He nodded, then looked a little sheepish. "You know I researched both you and Todd thoroughly this past summer."

Oh. She considered for a moment, glancing toward the

wolves out of the corner of her eye. "Does that mean you know my secrets?"

He shook his head. "I know your family has a title—a gift from the bears of the UK, and I know you've been estranged from them for eight years. I don't know why, but I'd assume it had something to do with Todd."

He was far too astute. "Right on all counts, but I'm not ready to talk about that yet. The point is I went from Lady Amanda, to Lord and Lady Ainsworth, because when Todd and I married, he had very grandiose plans, which meant again living a particular lifestyle."

"And you want more of the simple life?"

She nodded. "Definitely. And I want it to be new and fresh, which is why I asked everyone to call me Mandy. I'm reclaiming myself, in a way."

Warm fingers wrapped around hers, and he gave a brief squeeze before letting go. "Good for you."

He was so easy to talk with when he wasn't being bossy and growly. Although, she secretly liked that side of him too.

"And that's where my list comes in. Living in the pack house gave me a safe place to adjust to my new world, and now I feel as if the time is right for me to start going through the items I've noted."

"I'd say it was more than time. You deserve to enjoy some common, everyday pleasures."

He was being careful. Cautious, which was exactly what she needed to boost her confidence. "Would you like to see it? My list?"

The muffin in Justin's hand stuttered to a stop inches from his mouth.

"I'd be honoured." He put down the food and reached for the paper she slid across the table, glancing toward the wolf pair who were craning their necks in the hopes of catching a glimpse.

Justin made a show of holding the paper in the perfect way that they could almost, but not quite, see it.

Mandy laughed softly. "You're mean."

"Just wait. They're gonna find themselves a pair of eagle shifters to do their spying next," Justin whispered.

"I told you we should've made that pair of bird shifters stay in our territory," Evan grumbled as he got to his feet.

He and Amy waved goodbye then left. Mandy smiled in return, but Justin gave a dramatic evil-villain chuckle, as if they'd successfully vanquished an opponent.

"They mean well," Mandy pointed out.

"Wolves are the biggest busybodies."

Then he focused his attention on the list for real, his smile widening as he went down some of the items. "You wild woman. I don't know if you can do some of these unsuper—"

Yes, it was easy to tell the instant he hit the section of her list that ventured into naughty territory. She had the list memorized, she'd read over it so often, and partway down the page, it read...

take a painting class

camp in an RV

go snowmobiling

give a blowjob

go fishing for salmon in bear form

Justin's smile slowly faded, and his grip on the paper tightened briefly before he took a deep breath then consciously relaxed.

He folded the paper then put it back on the table as he met her gaze. "Who the hell do you...?"

She raised a brow, and his words died off, his eyes

flashing hot before he dragged himself under control and tried again.

"I mean, there's no damn way... Wait..." His mouth opened and closed a few times as he struggled to find the right words.

She waited patiently. He dragged in a deep breath then let it out as if he were blowing out a candle somewhere on the next table over.

"Mandy?"

"Yes?"

He cleared his throat. "I would like to offer to help you with your list."

Which was exactly what she hoped he'd say. "Lovely. On one condition."

"Anything," he swore, his tone ragged and one step from out of control.

She might want to move on and be independent, but there were items she needed a companion to complete. She'd been watching Justin closely for the last while. "If you want to help me with some things on the list, you have to help me with *all* the things on the list."

His lips twitched before he broke into a massive smile. "You're trying to scare me away, but it's not going to work."

"On the contrary, I'm really hoping a big, strong, *handsome* fellow like you isn't scared off that easily."

Justin's smile widened. "You think I'm handsome?"

"And strong." She nodded. "Oh...and sexy."

He beamed.

It was her turn to take a deep breath and hope for the best. Talk about pushing too far, too fast—

She knew he liked her, but was her next demand going to be too much? There was only one way to be sure, and it was better now than later when she'd just be hurt or disappointed.

She looked him in the eyes. "Justin, the things I want to do might seem ordinary and silly, but this relationship..."

Oh boy.

He smiled encouragingly, catching her hand in his again and carefully squeezing her fingers. "Go on. I won't think poorly of you if you say it wrong."

A warm, happy glow blossomed inside as that tiny seed of hope she'd held tucked away inside was finally allowed to sprout. Uncertainty clouded her future—this new life could vanish in an instant, and she had to take advantage of every moment.

She spoke softly, trusting him to understand what she meant to say, even if she screwed up the words. "I don't expect you to follow along behind me like a trained puppy, but I need to warn you I'm going to be selfish and expect you to *not* take control. I've had control out of my hands for so long, it's time I called the shots."

He leaned back in his chair as much as was possible in the tiny space he'd been allotted. "I'll try my best," he promised, "as long as you remember I'm a hardheaded bear. When I screw up, you'll need to kick me pretty hard."

"I can do that."

He wiggled in his chair uncomfortably. "I should warn you, I might have an issue with giving up control in the bedroom."

A delicious shiver raced over as he mentioned *bed.* "We'll cross that bridge when we get to it," she promised.

"When do we start?"

"How about right now?" She checked her watch. "In about thirty-five minutes."

3

———

*J*ustin had glanced at her sheet of paper, but honestly, he'd been more than a little distracted by the items he discovered toward the bottom of the page.

The first one that caught his eye and made him do a double take was *give a blow job*, and after that...

After that...

Good grief, was it *really* reasonable to expect him to remember anything that had come before or after that point on the page?

Which was why he wasn't sure what he was in for at the moment, other than she'd told him to bring a swimsuit and meet her at the Canada Games Centre.

He was smart enough to put two and two together and figure they were going in the pool, but when he strode onto the deck and discovered pumping music and a gaggle of women of all ages, it was only memory of the dirty things on the list that kept his feet moving forward.

Mandy reached to take his towel. "Right on time."

He took an up-and-down glance, appreciating how her

one-piece swimsuit hugged her curves. "I've never done one of these before," he admitted.

"Since that was kind of the point, that makes two of us." She dropped his towel on top of hers then guided him toward the ladder. "I think if we stand in the back that will help."

His warning instincts shot to high. It seemed every eye in the place was on them, which was probably true. The female population vastly outnumbered the men. All the lifeguards but one were women, and the lone male was admiring him more than Mandy, which simultaneously made Justin happy and wary.

"Everybody ready to shake it up?" The woman on the deck shouted the question, clapping her hands as she bounced enthusiastically.

A loud response roared back from the women in the pool.

Justin examined the Aquasize instructor a little closer, positive he'd seen her before—probably a wolf by how high energy she was. Before he could figure it out, Mandy was guiding them through the water to a spot in the back corner.

The class began, a surging wave of energy.

This was so not-his-thing, but after a few jumps and twirls, a single peek to his side showed Mandy was grinning from ear to ear as she splashed through the instructions, half a step behind at times, and he let his amusement rise.

A sense of rhythm wasn't her strong suit.

She twisted to face him, the rosy glow in her cheeks and her satisfied smile all the reward he needed as she wiped water from her eyes. He didn't even have to ask if she was having fun.

It was clear, and happy looked good on her.

"Lift those knees, ladies..." the instructor's gaze jumped

to him, "...and *gentleman*. Get those hands in the air, and let's make some noise."

Perhaps if he hadn't lived at the pack house for the past couple months the pandemonium would have been more of a shock, but as it was, Justin found himself moderately amused as he willingly went through the motions.

He was watching the instructor prance back and forth on the deck, toes rising in the air as she did a series of high kicks that he attempted to copy when a sudden splash hit him on the side of the face.

Justin snapped his gaze to the left, but Mandy was energetically moving to the beat, eyes fixed forward.

He got back into the rhythm just in time for another wave to hit, this one perfectly timed with him taking a big breath, which was the equivalent of having his head shoved underwater. He coughed and sputtered as he glanced again to the side.

Mandy was busy with her high kicks, focused intently on the instructor.

It was too unlikely of a scenario to be an accident.

The third time he turned just as the splash hit to discover Mandy grinning widely, her hands cupped together after tossing a load of water his direction.

Her mouth opened in an O of surprise as he marched closer to tower over her.

"Really?" he demanded.

She ducked down just far enough to suck up a mouthful of water before standing on her toes and hitting him full in the face with it.

She wanted to play it that way? Fine by him. He picked her up, careful to keep his grip light as he lifted her high and sent her flying into the open water to their right.

Mandy landed with a squeal and a splash, disappearing

under the surface to come up sputtering and laughing at the same time.

They grinned at each other.

"Hey. No horseplay."

Justin and Mandy glanced guiltily at the lifeguard standing in judgment over them.

"I'm so sorry," Mandy offered. "I...slipped."

Justin bit back a snicker as the guard gave them both dirty looks before walking away.

They were both on their best behavior as they got back into the class.

When all the bumping and jumping was over, Mandy slid next to him. "Hot tub?"

Oh, he could do that. Although, he'd really prefer if they were heading to a private hot tub where clothing would be optional instead of here with all the humans around.

He consoled himself by letting her climb out of the swimming pool first, enjoying how her hips swayed as she made her way up the ladder. The fabric of her suit clung to her as she turned and waited until he joined her.

They stepped down into the heated water together, and Justin let out a sigh of happiness.

"That wasn't so bad," he told her.

"It was fun. And we didn't even get thrown out of the class." Mandy batted her lashes.

He snorted. "Not for a lack of trying. Brat."

"Hey, we successfully accomplished one task. Maybe we should put 'get in trouble' on my list so we've got more incentive to follow through."

She pushed him ahead of her to the bench, and Justin settled in place, shoulders rising out of the water as he watched her and wondered what she was going to do next to drive him crazy.

~

THEY SAT SIDE-BY-SIDE, the force of the bubbling water enough to push her toward the middle of the pool.

"You don't have enough weight to keep yourself in one place," he teased as she threatened to float away completely. She didn't expect the hand that crept over her back before wrapping around her waist, and Mandy tensed.

Justin pulled his hands away immediately, holding them at the surface of the water. "Sorry."

She shook her head. "You didn't do anything wrong," she said firmly. "I'm a little jumpy, that's all."

She put her feet flat on the bottom until her shoulders rose above the surface of the water, increasing her weight so she could make her way back to the sidewall. More people were joining them, and the small, circular pool became crowded.

A man who'd been swimming lengths joined the crowd, and Justin tensed. Mandy glanced at him, but there seemed to be no reason—

Oh. He was was fighting to stop from putting himself as a buffer between the stranger and Mandy.

She moved instinctively to ease him, pressing herself against his side. "Lift your left arm," she murmured. "I need something to hang on to."

He chuckled as he raised his elbow to the surface, and she slipped her arms around it, pressing her torso against his triceps. Her knees bumped against his thigh, and the entire time the motion of the water rubbed her against him...

A low noise escaped before he choked it off in mid-rumble.

Mandy glanced down, and that's when she realized men's swimsuits were absolutely zero help when it came to hiding erections. Big, bear-sized erections, and if she wasn't in the pool and all, she'd have had to find an excuse to explain the sudden rush of heat and moisture that hit between *her* legs.

He wasn't getting out of the pool anytime soon, not unless it turned icy cold, which wasn't likely.

Distraction was needed.

She rested her chin on his shoulder to speak. "I made us an appointment this afternoon at the art studio."

He leaned toward her. "Sounds fun."

"We'll see. Are you sure you won't get in trouble with me taking over your schedule like this?"

He shook his head. "I'm pretty much my own boss unless Tyler is around."

Which reminded her all over how confused she'd been to discover Justin had remained in Whitehorse. Glad—but confused. "I thought you were a bodyguard. How come he's gone, and you're not guarding?"

"Because he left on his honeymoon, and I was smart enough to know I wasn't welcome." He turned and offered her a secret grin. "He's safe. I've got a surveillance team on him at all times."

"That's sneaky." And made her a little nervous. "He doesn't know?"

"Oh, trust me, he knows I've got someone watching him, even though he doesn't know exactly who, but it's not the same as having his best friend watching him make goo-goo eyes at his new wife. One of my jobs is to keep him safe, well, him and Caroline now, and he's not allowed to argue with what it takes to get the job done."

She nodded, but it still made her think back to less-than-happy times. "That was my least favourite part of being married to Todd. With all his political aspirations, it always felt as if someone was watching me." A shiver escaped in spite of the heated water.

"It's not always pleasant to think about," he agreed "but it is the price of being a public figure."

He leaned his head back on the pool ledge and closed his eyes, and she got to stare to her heart's content.

Justin's dark good looks were eye-candy to add sweetness to the ordinary, simple pleasure she'd already experienced. The heat of the water buoyed her as she considered his willingness to come jump up and down and basically make a fool of himself.

She held onto his arm, using him as an anchor.

People were entering and exiting the pool all the time, but they gave Justin and her a wide berth, especially as a rumble rose from his hairy chest. At first it was low enough to be a tickle in her ears, but as she checked him more carefully, the rumble deepened. Grew more intense, the kind of noise she could imagine him making as he ran his hands over her skin. Petting and caressing her. Pressing his lips to the spot under her ear that drove her wild as he stroked a hand up the inside of her...

Okay, that was letting her imagination run away a bit too far.

He groaned—an intensely sexual noise, as if he was in the middle of a wild fantasy similar to the one she'd been enjoying, and in spite of everything inside her that wanted to keep listening, she wiggled higher until she could lay her hand on his chest.

"Justin," she whispered urgently.

He cracked an eye open. "Had enough?"

Not nearly enough if her libido had anything to say about it. But she nodded then offered a warning. "You're making...noises."

Dirty noises. Wonderful, panty-wetting, makes-me-want-to-melt noises.

He shuffled back to a sitting position, blinking when he discovered only one person remained in the hot tub with them. An older woman. Human, but obviously alert to the nuances of the shifter world as she glanced between the two of them, a mischievous smile twisting her lips.

"Y'all planning on coming to Aquasize on a regular basis?" she asked with a grin. "Because I think my ticker got a better workout watching you two for the last few minutes than it did during the entire workout."

Mandy had no idea what to say in response.

Justin offered the old woman a wink.

She returned it enthusiastically. "You go getter', boy. If I were only twenty years younger."

"I'd have to be twenty years younger to keep up with you," Justin returned.

A smile drifted in unbidden as Mandy exited the tub and waited for Justin to join her.

"Flirt," she teased as they walked side by side toward the dressing rooms.

"My ego likes a little stroking," he confessed. He picked up her towel and draped it around her shoulders.

The offer to stroke parts of him *other* than his ego hovered on her lips. Mandy hurriedly tossed out different words. "Meet you on the other side?"

"Since that's my only option, sure."

She set the shower as cold as she could stand it,

excusing the need to cool off on the hot tub and not a reaction to being around Justin while letting her fantasies run rampant.

Only when she opened her locker all sexy thoughts vanished—

Something was off.

Mandy checked her things, but it seemed they were all there. Money, ID, credit cards. Her clothes and shoes were untouched, and there was no scent she could point out, but then her sniffer wasn't the best, and with the chlorine in the air and shampoo and soap wafting by, she was left with a lingering sense of uneasiness, and nothing more.

Maybe...she was missing her watch? But she couldn't be sure she'd even worn it today, after waking in a new place all excited to get together with Justin.

She dressed quickly, suddenly needing to be next to the big protective bear and let him reassure her that nothing was wrong.

Nothing could be wrong, because she'd already survived too many days where things went wrong. Those days were in her past...

Oh, how she hoped they were in her past.

4

———

$\mathcal{J}$ustin waited outside the change rooms, nodding politely as other members of the class left. Some giggled as he dipped his head, but he barely gave any of the other women more than a passing glance, his focus fixed on the door Mandy should slip out of soon.

The bit of teasing between him and Mandy during the class had been nowhere near where he wanted to go, but the sweet, innocent interaction had felt right, as long as she didn't plan to keep them going at that pace for another couple of months.

He'd hurriedly showered and dressed while considering hard. She'd been through a lot, he knew that. And for a human woman it would probably take a long time to recover from how she'd been treated. But as a shifter, she'd already made it clear she was taking steps to move on.

She never should've suffered in the first place, and the urge to track down her ex flared again. Justin let it go and refocused on the most important thing, which was him and Mandy, and finding how they fit.

More ways than one.

It was too much temptation for one man to bear, or maybe it was too much temptation for one bear to handle without losing control of his man. The woman he wanted with a desperate need had sat next to him clothed in a scrap of fabric he could ball into one fist and barely notice it was there.

Justin leaned against the wall and rested his head back, closing his eyes as he attempted to think of terrible things to get his cock to deflate.

The problem was, with his eyes closed it was too easy to drift back to the hot tub, the sweet scent of her filling his head. The scenario slipped farther in his mind than it had in reality as he imagined her straddling him, resting her hands on his shoulders as their bodies slid together.

He forced his attention back to the here and now, willing his body to stop tormenting him.

When she finally joined him, Mandy's expression seemed dazed, and he jerked to attention. "What's wrong?"

She shook her head. "I don't know for sure. I *thought* I wore my watch, but it wasn't in the locker. I was looking around to see if I'd left it anywhere. Sorry it took me so long—"

Justin went on high alert. "You think someone stole it?"

"Or I'm mistaken, and it's back at my new place." She offered him a sheepish smile. "I'm not completely settled in yet. It's very possible I didn't follow my usual routine."

He didn't want to alarm her, so he didn't argue other than insisting they stop at the front desk where she left a description in case it was turned in to the lost and found.

Out in the parking lot, though, he couldn't help himself. "Since we're both going the same direction, how about we get down to one vehicle?"

Mandy considered the suggestion. "I suppose that makes sense."

"Be nice to the environment," he teased.

"I insist on paying for gas." She tossed him her keys.

Okay, that was better than he'd expected.

With all the stalking—correction—with all the *casually happening to notice every single detail about her in a totally not stalker-ish creepy way* he'd done, he'd figured she was going to insist on driving. He didn't really care if it was her Jeep or his, as long as they were together in one vehicle.

He'd text one of the Takhini pack and get them to grab his vehicle from the swimming-pool parking lot. "What time is our art class, and do you have anything you need to do before then?"

Mandy asked to stop at the store, and he followed along happily as she selected a few things, pretending he was in dire need of some items himself. She strolled up and down the aisles wearing a contented expression, and he wasn't about to do anything to wipe that expression off her face.

Shopping was followed by lunch at another coffee shop, with sandwiches and pitcher-sized cups of coffee filled to the brim. It was brisk out, but both of them sat at their outdoor table in shirtsleeves, the cool air nowhere near enough to make their shifter blood need a jacket.

He let his gaze drift over her, admiring the bare skin he wanted to lick.

Mandy made a low noise of pleasure at the first bite into her sandwich, and a shiver raced up his spine.

He really had to stop connecting everything she did with sex. It was tough, because everything about her appealed to him on a completely animal level as well as fascinating his mind.

She daintily held her sandwich out. "You have to try this."

He wrapped his fingers over hers and took a bite, overlapping where she'd already tried it, and he swore, as good as the sandwich was, the only thing he could taste was her.

"Delicious," he said with a nod.

She offered a beautiful smile before turning to her phone to check messages and sipping her coffee quietly.

The trip to the art studio took barely ten minutes, and Justin found himself at the throwing wheel next to hers as he struggled to turn his clay into something less lump-like.

Mandy listened intently to the instructor, hands slipping over the rugged clay block, effortlessly smoothing the solid piece into a tall thick rod, her wet fingers working the clay up and down and up—

Shit. He was hard again.

Justin wiggled uncomfortably, the move knocking his hands too hard into his spinning lump of nothing, setting one edge out of kilter. The messy tower toppled to one side, deflated.

If his friend Tyler were here now, he'd be making comments about limp dicks.

Mandy glanced his direction, not even paying attention to the vase rapidly forming under her hands. Talented hands. Hands he really wanted all over him...

He bit back a groan as his clay folded in on itself again.

"You need a lighter touch," she teased.

Do not say it. Do not say it.

His mouth wasn't as smart as his brain. "I'm used to stroking a little rougher," he growled, his throat tight with lust.

Her eyes widened briefly before she snapped her head

back to her pottery wheel, but she was still smiling.

By the time they put their projects on the side table to be left for firing, he'd gotten control of his body, willingly following Mandy to the sinks to wash their fingers clean.

"That was fun." Her satisfied sigh ended with amusement. "Although, I'm not quite sure what you're going to do with an ashtray. You don't smoke."

"I'll give it to Tyler and Caroline as a wedding gift. He'll have to keep it in some prominent place in their house."

She laughed. "You should paint pink daisies on it before it gets fired."

"Pink daisies?"

"With tiny blue forget-me-nots, or a giant sunflower in the bottom."

They grinned at each other like conspirators. The mood between them fun and lighthearted. Then she changed the moment by clicking her tongue.

"Stand still. You've got clay on you."

She took a wad of napkins and wet one corner. Slipping next to him and catching hold of his shirt front, she tugged until he leaned over, his head on level with hers. Then she proceeded to carefully swab the mud from his cheek and temple.

"You were getting into your work," she teased.

"Anything worth doing is worth doing right." He caught her fingers loosely in his, bringing her knuckles close enough he could press a kiss to them. "Thank you."

Mandy blinked rapidly before clearing her throat and all but running from the room. Justin grinned hard as he followed her.

They sat in comfortable silence on the journey back into Whitehorse until he pulled her Jeep to a stop into the parking space where she was staying.

Comfortable, but the silence had given him plenty of time to run through ideas for what came next.

~

Justin was out his door and around to her side of the jeep before she could protest. Helping her down and keeping hold of her hand.

"I don't want to overstay my welcome, but would you like to sit for a while?"

Mandy's heart rate increased, then increased again. They'd spent nearly the entire day together, which meant if she was going to take the space and time she'd promised herself, the next move *should* be saying good night.

He spoke again before she could tell him that. "You have a lot of things on your list, and I thought it might be fun if we mix them up a little. Unless you're determined to start at number one and work your way straight through."

Oh boy. "No, I'm not a purist. I even read series out of order," she confided.

What the heck. Mandy caught him by the fingers, tugging him down the path outside the apartment. She hadn't had time to explore the entire place yet, but she'd seen this while looking out her window that morning.

A pretty park bench sat on the top of a rise overlooking the Yukon River. The trees and bushes arranged around the solid wooden structure formed a partially secluded oasis. They would still be in public, and people could see them from the walking path just below, but unless someone wanted to make their way up the hill, it was a lovely, isolated location.

She settled on the bench, eyes fixed forward as she pretended to admire the view.

Justin sat beside her, a soft chuckle rumbling up from his big bear-chest. "That was a contented sigh."

Mandy blinked, glancing up in surprise. "Did I sigh? It wasn't a bad thing—I'm very content. It's been a good day, and your company has been wonderful."

"I'm yours to command."

It was said so seriously, but for some reason her brain jumped back to the kids' movie from years earlier, and all she could think of was Justin as a big blue genie, offering to fulfill her every wish.

"About my list..."

Justin stretched an arm along the back of the bench, his biceps brushing her shoulder. "Yes?"

It was fun to know she could tease this big man. She felt completely safe around him, although building that trust was why it had taken until now for her to make a move. "You didn't really think I wanted to do everything in exactly the order it was written?"

He shrugged. "You're the boss, but no. I figured you kinda compartmentalized things and wrote them down as they came to you. All sorts of crafts, all sorts of sports..."

"...all sorts of sex."

Justin grinned.

"It's taken me a while to work up my courage." Maybe this confession would help him understand. "I wasn't just waiting for the divorce to go through. It's taken two months to decide I deserved to find myself. And I have all sorts of big ideas, but even then I might have times where something seems like a good idea, but I'll have to back off or slow down." She laid a hand on his thigh, the thick muscles quivering under her fingers. "But I trust you," she said softly. "I hope you know that means an awful lot."

His expression changed as she spoke. His initial

amusement and sexual interest turned, and what she witnessed on his face now was far more serious and solemn and completely filled with what she desperately needed to see—respect.

"I don't ever want to break that trust," he assured her.

So perfect, and so enticing, and suddenly she'd had enough talking.

Very clearly stated on her list was the desire to make out somewhere not completely private, and there was no better time than now. The arm he'd placed on the back of the bench curled around her cautiously as if he were cradling a priceless work of art. She lifted her chin and leaned toward him as he leaned toward her and their lips met.

A kiss. Their first.

As a first kiss it was pretty perfect—tender and sweet. His lips moved over hers slowly as she considered what he tasted like. What it felt like.

What it did to her insides...

For the record—surprisingly earth-shattering, considering they had less than two inches of body contact going on.

Inside, a mixer was churning on high speed. A red-hot brand heated in her belly, and lower. Her sex tingled and tightened as he took the kiss deeper, teasing her lips with his tongue until she opened to him and breathed a sigh.

He captured the sound, the arm around her body sliding downward until his hand rested on her hip. His grip tightened for a moment before relaxing, but she was the one who leaned into him farther, letting the heart-fluttering impact of his mouth do its job.

She moaned as he kissed her harder, not stopping as he lifted her into his lap in one swoop. Mandy was airborne for a second before settling against the heat of his body, his legs solid under hers. His erection a rock against her hip.

She lifted her hands to his chest and pressed back gently.

Justin instantly opened space between them, smiling down at her. "Oops. How did you get there?"

A laugh escaped. "I can't imagine. Maybe kissing pixies live by this bench, and they magically lifted me."

He tilted his head from side to side for a moment before agreeing. "Seems the only logical explanation to me."

Mandy slid her palms up his chest, over the wall of muscle until she could drape her hands over his shoulders, staring into his face. "That was nice. The kissing."

One brow shot upward. "Nope."

She hesitated. "It *wasn't* nice?"

"Hell, no," he said with a determined shake of his head. "If that's how you're going to go around describing my kissing skills, my reputation with the wolves will end up in shreds."

"I understand." She trickled a finger over his lips as she pretended to consider their options. "Perhaps we'd better try again while I consider better adjectives."

"Only for that reason."

A cold wind swept past, but Mandy was surrounded by a bubble of heat. Justin's body under her a flaming furnace. He kept himself in control, though, the power and strength of his passion tightly leashed. His restraint allowed her to concentrate on everything else as she got lost in their kiss.

She was trying to think of a description that would impress the wolves, really she was, but words were blurry, fuzzy things that seemed to bubble and fizz in her brain in an unknown foreign language.

The next time they pulled apart she was seeing stars.

His hands firmly grasped her hips, her fingers were buried in the short hair at the back of his neck.

She sucked for air before managing to speak. "Wow."

Justin grinned. "Much better."

It was tempting to go farther. To ask him up to her apartment, and maybe move on to another item on the list, but something inside told her she wasn't quite ready.

She might be willing now, but if things went too far, too fast and she had to call for a stop, that would be worse than sticking to her original plan of going slowly.

She crawled off his lap and straightened her clothing, glancing up to discover he was grinning.

"What?"

He just shook his head, holding out a hand. Their fingers linked as he escorted her to the security door.

"Do you know your plans for tomorrow? Because..." He cleared his throat. "I'll just make a fool of myself once and for all. I want to be with you, Mandy. I want you to let me know what you need a hand with, but I can't help myself. If you don't call me, I'll come looking. And it's not because I want to control you, it's because I want to be with you."

His confession sent a shiver skipping over her skin. It wasn't a shiver of fear like Ainsworth had put in her, but Justin's admission was borderline bossy, and she wasn't ready for that. She wasn't ready to be even remotely thrilled at how much he seemed to care.

The line between obsession and caring was too raw in her memory.

"I'll call you," she promised, stepping inside the building.

He waited until the door closed, the lock clicking firmly shut between them. The six or seven paces it took to get to the elevator, she could sense he was watching, his gaze fixed on her until the doors closed and blocked them from each other's view.

She leaned her forehead against the wall and let out a long, slow breath, willing her heart to slow its frantic pace.

"Oh, Mandy. He's a fine one, but you don't need to rush," she chastised herself as the elevator doors opened with a soft *ping*. She slipped down the hallway to her suite and used the access card. The door swung open.

Mandy stood in the doorway, frozen, nerve endings tingling a warning.

Once again, something seemed off, but she couldn't tell exactly what. The sensation of someone having been where they shouldn't have been struck like it had at the pool, but even stronger, and the edge of uncertainty was enough to have her stepping back and pulling the door closed silently.

She headed down the hallway rapidly, her heart racing. The urge to message Justin hit, immediate and strong. And it wasn't a bad idea, but was it the *best* idea?

Justin would willingly protect her—there was no doubt about that—but if she was overreacting, she didn't want him to think she was going to constantly jump at shadows. Maybe the wolves had sent someone to the apartment for some reason. It was a plausible explanation. It was...

But she wasn't going to be stupid and assume everything was okay.

Don't think—act.

Mandy took out her phone and sent a text to another she knew she could trust implicitly.

Amy. I think someone's been in my apartment.

Mandy took the stairs, clutching the railing to slow herself as she hurried downward. She rushed outside and glanced around.

Keeping their animal natures secret in the midst of a

mostly human city had made the development of certain items logical in the shifter community. Since the Takhini pack owned the apartment, they ought to have shifters stay there, ergo, there should be a place nearby where she could cache her clothes.

She found the box elegantly disguised as a decorative post office box. For all she knew the top half of it was used for snail mail, but the bottom held a door that slid open to reveal two private compartments. The back of the box was set just deep enough into the trees that she could strip down quickly and stay out of sight.

Standing in the nude, Mandy placed all her things into the hidden space. That included her phone, but she would have no way to answer it within seconds anyway.

Then she closed the door and applied her thumbprint to the small pad, thoroughly impressed with the Takhini pack's high-tech security.

The momentary distraction gave her something else to think about other than how scared she was—unreasonably scared, probably, but with her history, unreasonable became reasonable enough in a heck of a hurry.

She crouched low and willed the change to come over her, limbs and torso rearranging themselves quickly to her other form. Her animal side was more powerful and less delicate than her human form, but still susceptible to tranquilizer guns of human animal enforcement.

Staying out of sight was imperative. Mandy wasn't trying to do anything other than keep safe.

She slipped quietly through the trees until she had a good vantage point of the back door, her apartment windows visible above her. Silently she lay on her belly and waited.

5

___

*J*ustin wasn't even through the doors at the pack house when he bumped into Evan racing the other direction.

The Alpha wolf put a hand on his shoulder and turned him forcibly, all but spinning him out the door toward the parking lot.

Justin was in no mood to be tolerant of impulsive wolf behavior. "What the—?"

"We just got a text from Mandy. She needs us."

That was enough to cause a total change of attitude and plans. In a split second, Justin was charging alongside the wolf even as he slipped a hand into his pocket and pulled out his phone to check for messages.

Nothing.

An unwelcome sense of disappointment kicked in along with rising concern, and he hit one of his autodial-preprogrammed texts and sent off a secret message.

"What did she say?" Justin demanded as they ignored their vehicles and ran full speed down the path between the buildings, headed to the apartment faster on foot using shortcuts than driving and parking.

They might have been moving rapidly, but Evan barked out a warning instead of an answer. "Advice for you."

Justin bit back the growl that wanted to escape.

The wolf Alpha led his boisterous and seemingly borderline-out-of-control ragtag crew, but he did it in a way that meant very few arrests or deaths in the shifter community he cared for, which was a powerful statement in itself.

His advice shouldn't be tossed aside, no matter how much Justin questioned his timing. "What?"

"You're ready to roll in there, guns blazing. Or you're going to do the exact opposite of what your gut is telling you, and you'll pull your punches and control the beast because you don't want to scare her." They were already only a block away from where Justin had left Mandy when Evan laid a hand on his arm, pulling him to a rapid walk from their all-out sprint. "Either one of those would be a mistake. I don't envy you the balancing act, but learn from my mistake. When Amy and I were dealing with our past, I didn't take it seriously enough how much she needed me to be *me*, as well as listen to her concerns."

"This isn't the time for a lecture," Justin snapped, frantic to keep moving.

"We'll be there in thirty seconds," Evan promised, "but this is *important*, man. I didn't get my kick-in-the-ass until I'd already screwed things up, so from one Alpha male to another, listen to what she *needs*, but don't hold back."

"Fine." Justin stored the advice away for later, rushing forward at Evan's side as they closed in on the tall apartment house at the edge of town.

Evan took a deep breath then snapped a finger toward

the trees. "Mandy's over there, in her bear form. You wanna talk to her while I go check out the apartment?"

Justin nodded at Evan's retreating back before peering into the darkness, trying to spot the shifted form of the woman who'd sent his heart racing. "Mandy? Hey, pretty lady. Everything's going to be okay."

He stepped forward again, following her scent to her hiding place. He paused at the edge of the clearing, offering a reassuring smile when he finally spotted her in the shadows.

Appreciation rose for her skillful camouflage because she had a more difficult task than most. Justin had known she was unusual, but this was the first time he'd actually seen her animal form.

Her fur was the delicate mixture of white, grey and silver that was often mistaken at first glance for polar bear, but was instead the marker of a member of Kodiak Island. Ghost bears—rare and beautiful.

"I don't know what spooked you, but I'm very impressed," he admitted. She'd done a great job hiding. "If Evan hadn't told me where to start looking, you'd still be hidden, and that can't be an easy task with your white fur."

Mandy rose to all fours, coming beside him to lean her shoulder and head against his leg.

She was so small it only made sense to kneel at her side. "Why don't you stay in that form," he suggested. "Evan will be back in a minute, and we can figure out what you'd like to do at that point."

She nodded then dropped her hind quarters to the ground. Her head tilted back, and he followed the line of her gaze to the upper apartment where a light had just come on, the tall form of Evan clear behind the windows.

"He's in there now."

While they waited Justin thought hard about the advice the wolf had given him. What he wanted at this moment first and foremost was to grab Mandy and head for the hills. Whatever the hell was going on, he wanted her by his side— but she'd specifically asked for him not to take over.

Which meant he had to get her to change her mind, because he wasn't changing his. Not if she was in danger.

He put an arm around her shoulders, her fur soft under his hands. He wanted to shift and join her, protecting and comforting her the way his bear itched to do.

Fortunately, or unfortunately, he was distracted by his phone vibrating in his pocket.

"Someone's definitely been in here." Evan started without preamble. "A couple someones."

"Your pack?"

"Nope, bear. No one I recognize, either. Which means it's not her ex, but that doesn't mean it's not someone connected to him."

Justin held back the curses that wanted to escape. "Suggestions?"

He fully expected for the wolf to order him to bring her back to the pack house, but instead, he surprised Justin.

"Get her out of town," Evan said. "If you need help, let me know. Otherwise she hasn't even unpacked. I can grab her bags and be down there in a few minutes."

Talk about a juggling act. This was exactly what he wanted. Mandy at his side.

But it was exactly what he didn't want—control taken from her, with him thrust into the position of protector.

It was a good thing he wasn't only strong and handsome, as she'd pointed out, but very, *very* smart.

Justin lifted her chin until her gaze met his.

"Here are the options as I see them," he said clearly.

"Someone has been in your apartment. You figured that out —well done—now tell me what you want to do." He held up a finger. "You can go back to the Takhini pack house, but until we know who was in the apartment, you could be bringing trouble on our friends. Number two"—another finger rose—"you leave completely. If there's somewhere you think you'd be safe, like back home with your family, we'll go there."

Her eyes flickered as she took in his words.

"Yes, no matter where you go, I'm going with you. And the third option is you and I take off, but *I'll* set the agenda. This could all be some kind of overreaction on our part, but I have the means and ways to keep you safe. And while I keep you safe, we're going to keep working on your list," he promised. "Because it's not right to let anyone steal another day from you."

She stared up at him as she considered the options he offered, the dark brown of her human pupils an even deeper shade in her bear form.

Then she surprised the hell out of him and shifted on the spot, a petite, fine-boned woman utterly naked before him as she knelt on the ground.

She raised her chin high. No fear marred her expression, only determination. "You're a bossy bastard," she said plainly, "but I can hardly argue with your logic. Only you should know—I'm tired of running."

He offered a quick nod of approval. "It's not running when you're going where you wanted to in the first place," he pointed out.

Mandy placed her hand in his and allowed him to guide her to her feet.

"But I'm in charge," she insisted. "I won't do anything stupid while you're protecting me, but..." She tapped her thumb to her chest just above her bare breasts. "I'm in charge of this. I know you won't forget that."

Justin took another cue from the Alpha of the wolves, bending over her fingers and pressing a kiss to her knuckles. "I think we're on the same page, my lady. Shall we get ready for our big adventure?"

MANDY DRESSED QUICKLY and was slipping on her shoes when the door to the apartment house opened and Evan Stone appeared, her suitcases in his hands. He turned unerringly to where she and Justin were walking toward him, waiting on the spot until they arrived. And like he'd done over the past couple months every time he'd greeted her, he put the suitcases down to come forward and offer a bracing hug, protective and familiar as a brother's touch.

She was impressed Justin held back his possessive instincts. His growl of annoyance was barely audible this time.

Evan stepped back with a smirk on his lips as he glanced Justin's way. "Sorry. It's not my fault I'm wired to protect."

"Right. Because hugs are so protective," Justin grumbled.

Mandy wanted information, not Alpha-male posturing. "Was someone in my apartment?"

All traces of Evan's amusement vanished. "At least two, new blood."

Her heart skipped a beat. "Then, thank you for everything you've done, but I'm getting Justin to take me away."

Evan nodded. "I'll send you a list of my contacts. If any

of them can help at any time, call in a favour. In the meantime, I'll get some of my best trackers in to figure out what we can about your visitors."

"Hopefully it's just somebody who was curious about what I've been doing since the bear conclave and elections." Mandy knew it was a reasonable explanation, just not a very plausible one.

Evan held a hand to Justin who shook it firmly. "Anything you need, bro. It's yours."

"I've got people around town. Someone will be in touch with you to let you know what's happening with the projects we're doing together."

The wolf chuckled. "I should've known you'd have backup plans and would be ready to leave at the drop of a hat. *Flash.*"

"Don't try to flatter me," Justin warned. "We both know there are backup plans to our backup plans at this point in our lives."

"Of course. That's what happens after you learn a few hard lessons about what happens when you're not prepared..." The wolf gave a rather pointed *look* in Justin's direction.

Mandy wasn't quite sure what they were talking about, but when Justin motioned for her to join him, she stepped forward.

He picked up both her suitcases, one under his arm and the other gripped in his large fingers, before offering his free hand.

"I can take care of one of my suitcases," she suggested. "Won't it be hard for you to protect me with both your hands full?"

"Good point." He moved instantly, dropping the smaller suitcase and extending the handle so she could roll it with her right hand as he took hold of her left hand again.

They were halfway down the block before she realized she hadn't officially said goodbye to Evan because she'd been too amused by Justin's elaborate manoeuvering to keep hold of her fingers.

"And how exactly is this better?" she asked. "You still have both hands full."

"Yeah, but I can throw the suitcase at anyone who threatens us, so it's a perfect weapon."

They walked at a brisk pace as he guided them down the well-lit main streets of town. Behind them, Evan lurked in the shadows, a wolfish tail, offering double the protection.

"I suppose we'll have people following us all the time?" Mandy asked.

"Not unless it becomes necessary. And if it does, you shouldn't even notice them if they're doing their job right." He gestured with their joined hands toward a side street, tugging her in the new direction. "I said I'd protect you, and I'll use whatever means necessary, but I hope you'll let me take care of the details. If you want me to tell you everything, of course I will, but..."

Since he'd done such a clever job making it clear her only real option was to trust him, it seemed foolishness on her part to make his job more difficult. "Tell me what I need to know, or if I have concerns, I'll ask. If necessary, just tell me *you've got it covered*, and I'll let it go at that."

They moved in relative silence for the next couple blocks. She concentrated as hard as possible on her surroundings, listening for danger, but there was nothing but the erratic noises that were always present at night in a city, no matter how small. Soon enough they were behind the pack house where Justin escorted her to a Land Rover, popping the back open and tossing her suitcases in before helping her up the steep step into the high vehicle.

He was around the truck and in the driver's seat almost instantly, and she remained quiet, her curiosity at high, until they were safely on the road heading south out of Whitehorse.

"This isn't your truck," she pointed out. A quick glance in the back proved her bags weren't the only ones there. "Are those *your* suitcases?"

He nodded, gaze fixed on the highway. "I texted my contact. He's loaning the Land Rover to us for a bit. Just in case our visitors have been hanging around the pack house for a while. They might know our vehicles, or have them bugged."

All the precautions felt over the top, but she held her tongue and refused to allow her protests to escape. If he thought it was necessary—

She'd said she would trust him, so until proven otherwise, that's what she was going to do. It would take less energy on both their parts if she weren't questioning all the time.

Mandy was in a full-on personal debate to decide if she should ask where they were going, or if that crossed the line, when he volunteered some information.

"It's going to be pretty clear which way we're going to anyone with half a brain. There are only three main routes out of Whitehorse that don't end in the middle of the bush, and no one is going to believe you're foolish enough to get yourself trapped on one of those."

"Right."

"You mentioned you wanted to go snowmobiling. Best place for that right now is farther north."

Mandy twisted in her seat to stare at him. "Seriously? We're really going to work on my list?"

"Well, not this instant, but sure."

She was one second away from protesting before deliberately slamming her lips shut. *I need to trust him. He knows what he's doing.*

She forced herself to relax back into the leather seat. "I've never driven a snowmobile."

A soft chuckle escaped him. "As you said, that's kind of the point. Don't worry, you'll have a ball. We'll give you a couple of lessons, and you'll be bombing around in no time."

"And there's enough snow?"

"Not in Whitehorse, not yet. But up on the mountain passes, and farther north, winter arrived a few weeks ago. We'll have to pick some routes carefully, but I've got a buddy who will give us a hand."

Curiosity struck again. "You said you texted a contact and they got the Land Rover ready. When? And when did he have time to pack bags for you?"

Justin flashed a grin at her. "I have a set of emergency codes preprogrammed into my phone. One touch, and they know what I expect them to do."

"You're the biggest boy scout I've ever met."

His grin widened. "Always prepared is a great motto."

Mandy turned her gaze forward and jerked in surprise, snapping up a finger to point out the front window. "*Bear.*"

"Right on time." Justin pulled off the highway onto a narrow gravel road as the black bear meandered off the main road and into the trees.

They drove not even a mile when the road turned a sharp corner and doubled back into a clearing. They were completely out of sight of the highway, mostly covered by dense trees. Justin parked beside what seemed to be a souped-up RV.

Mandy's confusion increased. Camping had been on her list, but the timing seemed odd. "Are we camping?"

"Here? No."

Justin was a font of information. *Not*.

She poked for more details. "I kind of figured the camping was going to happen in spring."

He was out the door and around by her side, helping her to the ground. "It's a pretty skookum camper. We'd be warm enough."

He guided her to the front of the camper, glancing down at his watch impatiently while Mandy moved toward the smoke-coloured windows in an attempt to peek inside.

A dark-skinned man rounded the front of the camper, walking toward them wearing nothing but a smile.

He was obviously the person Justin was waiting for, because instead of pouncing on the fellow, or shouting, Justin just let out an enormous sigh.

"Are you *really* planning on driving like that?"

The other man shrugged. "Clothes make me itch."

"Fine, your choice, but I'm not bailing you out if you get arrested." Justin turned to Mandy to offer introductions. "This is Dale. That's his Land Rover we were just in."

Dale offered a fancy bow, hand waving before him as he bent low toward her. "And 'tis my camper you'll be enjoying, as well. If there's anything else you need, you be sure to let me or my kin know. We're at your disposal, milady."

"Umm, thank you. If there's anything I can do in return..."

Dale's gaze jumped between her and Justin before settling on her again. "No favours required," he insisted.

He walked past them and climbed into the Land Rover.

"If you get pulled over, the RCMP are going to go ballistic on your bare bear ass," Justin warned.

Dale closed the door before rolling down the window and leaning out. "There's a pretty young lass on the department in these parts. If she pulls me over, I'm sure we can come to some better arrangement than me spending the night behind cold metal bars."

He offered a cheeky wink before backing the vehicle up and turning it around. A low layer of dust rose from under the tires as he drove slowly to disappear around the corner.

Justin guided Mandy to the camper and got her buckled in. "You can look around later. I want to get on the highway."

Mandy had a million questions buzzing in her brain, and burning curiosity seemed to be her go-to new status. "Dale is a very— Oh no! He's got our suitcases."

Instead of panicking or grabbing for his phone to call the other bear shifter back, Justin put the camper in gear and manoeuvered out of the trees, heading to the highway.

Where he turned east, returning to Whitehorse.

Justin glanced at her. "Dale will drop our bags off as soon as he's had a chance to run them under a bug scanner, just to make sure no one's left any surprises for either of us."

Wow. This was getting way more twisted and complicated than she'd expected. "So...are we camping in Whitehorse?"

"No. Too close to unknown factors. I've got a safe house for us where we can hide and have fun working on your list."

With everything that had been going on over the past hour, her list seemed unimportant, and yet it was clear Justin was determined to stick to his commitment.

Which made it easier for Mandy to relax and go with the flow. "You really do know what you're doing."

"I really do."

She adjusted the seat slightly so she could lean back farther, looking out the window as the lights of Whitehorse drew nearer.

6

andy tried her best to stay awake, but the smooth ride after the full day slowly toppled her into dreamland.

She felt wonderfully rested when sleep finally let her go. She woke up in a comfortable shifter-sized bed—i.e. big enough to hold her and an entire family of bears.

For one moment she held her breath in hopeful anticipation before rolling over to discover an empty space at her side. Disappointment that Justin wasn't with her made her think hard about what she wanted.

Their little excursion out of Whitehorse had been unplanned, but Justin was right. Even though she needed to stay safe that didn't mean she should be willing to give up on the next steps in her life.

Mandy rolled again. Satiny smoothness teased her skin as she slipped her legs over the edge of the bed. She glanced down at a familiar nightgown, then over at the side table where her suitcase sat open.

Faint memories returned. Justin bringing her into the apartment, laughing softly at her sleepy clumsiness before leaving the room to let her slip into her night clothes and under the covers.

Her clothes from the previous day were neatly folded on a nearby chair. She got dressed quickly, glancing around the comfortably established room with curiosity before making her way toward the door behind which a soft, repetitive noise trickled.

The floorboards were warm underfoot, and beautiful pictures of wild mountain scenery hung on the walls as she stepped quietly into the living space.

Justin stood behind the island counter, whisk in hand as he rapidly beat batter in an oversized bowl.

He offered a smile. "Good morning, sleeping beauty."

Mandy glanced at the clock on the wall oven. "Wow. It's nearly good afternoon."

"Ten o'clock isn't that late, and we've got no agenda. I figured you should sleep until you were done."

She settled onto the stool on the side opposite him. "What time did we get here?"

"About four in the morning."

Whoa. "I hope you slept."

"Enough. I can nap later if necessary. Let me finish this and get it in the oven, then I can show you around."

He poured the batter into muffin tins, expertly filling each one to the exact same level without pausing or spilling on the countertop.

His competence at so many things, big and small, astounded her, and reminded her all over again that there was so much she didn't know. So many basic life skills along with the recreational activities, and she was like a little child wandering into the big, wide world for the first time.

She considered the sensation in her gut carefully, pleased to discover it wasn't a lack of confidence or hopelessness that had settled in hard, but more a sense of anticipation for what she had to look forward to learning.

All in all, that was a far better realization than returning to the fear and separation from community that had been part of her life for so long.

Mandy found herself smiling happily as she waited for him to finish and put the tin in the oven.

Justin dusted the flour from his big hands. "Twenty-five minutes until breakfast, and after, we can go explore."

"You want to tell me where we are?"

He blinked. "My bad. We're in Chicken."

Mandy opened her mouth to answer him, but nothing seemed to come in answer to such a weird proclamation. "*Okay...*"

Justin laughed softly. "Let me clean up. Take a peek— there should be a great view of Main Street from there."

She followed his pointing finger to the edge of a floor-to-ceiling window, which with the lofted ceiling meant the curtain she pushed aside revealed a massive sheet of glass. The second-floor vantage gave her an unobstructed view, and she stared down excitedly.

It was like looking at a set for an old western movie. False fronted buildings sat along a rustic wooden boardwalk. The road was snow-covered dirt, or fine gravel, and glancing along the entire length of roadway, she didn't spot a single set of street lights.

The vehicles on the street were the only giveaway that they hadn't traveled back in time. Although the first truck she spotted was circa 1920s, the next was a sleek, modern Hummer that pulled up to the curb behind it.

The grocery store behind the vehicles had rows of produce displayed on wooden racks outside the door, and a man in overalls was clearing the boardwalk of snow with a pushbroom. A woman in skirts that brushed the bare boards strolled up with a parasol over her shoulder to examine the apples.

Mandy had never heard of the town, but this was beyond anything she'd expected. "Is there a reenactment society in town—?"

Her question died off in the middle as the doors of the Hummer opened, and two humans got out followed by a huge number of what at first glance looked like dogs. Mandy examined them closer, gasping in surprise as a couple in the group shifted to human form, standing naked on the street as they pointed in different directions, obviously debating which way to go first.

"Whoa."

Justin stood beside her, amusement in his voice as he answered. "Yes, it's a shifter town."

"Only shifters?"

He leaned forward, pointing to the opposite side of the street where a pair of wolverines marched shoulder to shoulder. "The rare human shows up, but they mostly pass straight through. We're in a very remote part of Alaska right now, and at this time of year especially, the only people here are the ones who belong."

Mandy gave in to temptation, leaning against the warmth of his body. "I've never seen anything like it."

"Most countries have a few shifter towns. Chicken is unusual in that it's got all sorts of types of shifters instead of only wolves, or cats, or whatever."

"And they don't fight?"

"Of course they fight." He stroked a hand down her arm. "They just make up faster than usual, and they tend not to tear the place apart, which is helpful."

"I don't like fighting."

He twisted her, and it was the most natural thing to slip into his arms. "Princess."

"Maybe, but I don't like violence or the political games. And I don't fight."

One brow rose, but he seemed completely focused on stroking her hair behind her ear. A quiet and intimate movement.

Suddenly, he stepped his feet wider and tugged her tightly against his body. "You fight yourself." He pointed between them. "You fight what comes naturally, like the heat between us."

True—until now. "Who said anything about fighting it any longer?"

Mandy melted against him as she tilted her head back to accept the kiss he offered. She pressed her palms to his chest and let the heat of his body wrap around her.

His touch remained gentle as he enticed all her senses, and she became more alert. As if she'd woken up, not just her body, but her entire self.

It was time for this. It was time to enjoy the attraction they felt, and she slid her hands higher until she could grasp behind his neck and pull him even closer.

Justin growled his approval, hands dropping to her hips before he easily lifted her in the air, not breaking contact between their mouths. He walked blindly away from the window, and she wasn't exactly sure where they were going because she was concentrating on how good it was to have him stroke their tongues together. How light and delicate she felt in his possessive grasp on her hips.

Heat rose in her body as he worked her over, playing. Teasing.

He settled her on a hard surface, and the next thing she knew his hands were pressing her legs farther apart.

"I want to taste you everywhere," he growled, need and desire powerfully clear in his voice.

She nipped at his lips, kissing lightly before withdrawing. Taunting him, taunting them both.

She'd have continued to play for a lot longer but he clearly had a different agenda in mind, because the next thing she knew she was naked from the waist down and Justin was on his knees before her. He dragged her hips forward to the edge of the counter and put his mouth to Ground Zero.

"Oh, *yes*."

He licked and stroked, fingertips sinking into her butt cheeks as he shifted her ever so slightly, changing pressure to direct the torment perfectly. Softer now as he eased up one side of her folds then down the other before gently tugging her clit. Small motions that increased in tempo and pressure until she was one second away from exploding.

And—he pulled back.

Her body stuttered to a stop.

"Justin," she complained.

He glanced up, a glint of amusement mixed with the fire in his eyes. "I'm not done. That was the appetizer. *Now* I'm ready to enjoy myself."

He slid a hand over her belly and upward, pressing on her torso until she was forced to lie flat on the countertop. Feet on the edge, her head resting on solid granite. She stared at the ceiling above her where a delicate chandelier of sparkling glass hung. Some of the jewel-like pieces were made of stained glass...

That's about when her vision began to blur, because now that he had her in the position he wanted, Justin went back to work, driving his tongue deep and sending her senses reeling.

Pressure increased as he slipped a finger into her sex, her aching flesh welcoming him as a shiver shot over her skin. He eased back then thrust again, over and over until she reached out and buried her fingers in his hair.

"You're not going anywhere," she ordered, desperately hoping he'd obey her, because if he didn't want to, there wasn't much she could do to stop him from moving.

Justin answered by licking more firmly, a second finger easing in with the first.

It'd been so long since she'd felt anyone's touch except her own, it was no wonder she was seconds away from climax. A few more strokes, a few more caresses and she'd be there.

But he didn't play fair, easing off the pressure just enough to make her complain vehemently.

He lifted over her, leaning one elbow on the island beside her as he gazed into her eyes, his fingers buried in her body. "I hate to rush, but sometimes we just need to get the job done. I bet you're pretty when you come."

It had to be his thumb circling over and over with slowly increasing pressure to her clit as he rubbed his fingertips inside her sex. The tension timed perfectly to drive her anticipation to the edge and then beyond, welcoming the orgasm as it shook her entire body. Her sex clamped down on his fingers, and she fought desperately to keep her eyes open, staring back as he hummed in approval as she lost control.

Justin truly was good at everything he put his hand to.

Every time she thought her body was done, he adjusted his fingers and drove her on. Waves struck like the ocean during a storm, each one breaking and crashing into the next until she collapsed bonelessly, unable to take anymore.

Justin eased his hand free as he leaned over her, the

hard length of his erection pressing against her leg. He didn't seem unhappy, though. Quite the contrary. He smiled before lifting his hand to his mouth and licking his fingers clean.

Mandy opened her mouth to say something, although she wasn't sure quite what was appropriate. A simple *thank you* seemed inadequate, but then the timer on the stove went off, and Justin pulled her to a sitting position before pressing a brief kiss to her lips.

"Stay right there," he ordered.

She was dazed enough to not care she was bare-assed naked, legs wide as she watched him be all-domestic and pull their breakfast from the oven.

There was no shame in what they'd done, although she really hoped she'd be able to do something for him in return soon.

JUSTIN DIDN'T CONSIDER himself good martyr material. He knew exactly what he liked, and he mostly managed to live in a way that pleased him. Comfortable surroundings were the norm, his time in the wolf pack house not withstanding. He rarely had to forgo creature comforts even in his role as bodyguard for Tyler.

But when it came down to it, he was willing to make whatever sacrifices were needed to meet his goals and complete the challenges of his day.

Only current and ongoing goal: keep Mandy safe and make her happy. In that order. If he could do both at the same time, all the better. The fact *making her happy* would involve sex as well as excursions?

Justin Cullinan was one contented bear.

Point in case—that morning bringing her pleasure had been the highlight of his past few days. He had no intention of rushing her, and if she needed more time, he'd give it to her. Yup, he was willing to provide all the oral sex she could handle.

Meanwhile he was focusing on the first part of the task, keeping her safe as she wandered town checking everything out, her fingers tangled in his. All talk of her to-do list had seemingly been forgotten, which was fine. Although he hoped she'd come back to it eventually, because he was looking forward to the more physical requirements, like when she decided it was time to move forward and finally put her hands on him intimately.

His cock rose at the thought, and he adjusted himself casually to a less painful position.

Mandy stood in front of the plaque that explained how the town got its name, laughing out loud when she reached the end. "That is something I would have done. My family used to tease me unmercifully for how poor my spelling was."

Justin shifted his body slightly to protect her from a group walking past in the opposite direction. "Face it, *Ptarmigan* would have made a great name for the town, but it isn't the easiest word to spell. But you think they would have picked something else completely."

"No, *Chicken* works perfectly—it's funny. Like... ptarmigans are arctic chickens, right?" Her nose wrinkled adorably. "Wait. *Are* there any ptarmigan shifters?"

"Probably," he said with a smile. "Only the gentler shifters tend to stay a little more isolated."

"For good reason, I suppose."

Justin shrugged. "Shifters are shifters. We're all tougher than humans, even those who don't have fur or sharp teeth.

And don't discount any of the wild kingdom—you ever been on the wrong side of an ordinary red-winged blackbird? Dangerous and territorial, even though they're small."

She shook her head then got distracted and pulled him into another shop where he waited for her to finish wandering the aisles, exclaiming over the pretty clothes and intricate knickknacks.

Utterly patient. Aching for more.

It was nearly two p.m. before her stomach grumbled loudly enough they both heard it. Mandy glanced down at her bare wrist before grabbing his to check his watch.

She twitched in surprise before turning to punch him playfully on the arm. "You're so bad. Why didn't you say it was so late? You must be starving."

"We ate a late breakfast," he told her. "I'm a big boy. I won't cry if I miss a meal."

Her gaze drifted over him, and her smile shifted to something far more along the lines of what he was hoping for.

"You *are* a big boy." She stepped closer, licking her lips as she leaned against him, her head barely to the middle of his chest. "Got any ideas of somewhere tasty you'd like to go?"

Back to the apartment and into bed?

No, wait. He better feed her first because once he got her into bed he wasn't letting her up. They'd need their strength. "I know just the place."

He untangled from her reluctantly, keeping a tight grip on her fingers to guide her down the street to the pub.

Mandy paused, tilting her head back to check out the nameplate above the window. "Northern Lights *Theater*?"

"NLT is *the* place in Chicken," he promised.

It took a second for his eyes to adjust from the bright

daylight outside to the dimmer lighting in what had been an old theater lobby.

Mandy blinked hard, glancing in open-mouthed wonder at the majestic trappings decorating the walls and painted ceiling as Justin guided her toward the seating area at the bar mostly on memory. He didn't think twice before catching hold of her hips and once again lifting her into the air, placing her on one of the tall gilded chairs in front of the bar counter.

She tilted her head and gave him a warning look, but when she didn't say anything, he settled himself in, lightly resting an arm along the back of her chair.

Mandy leaned forward to admire the bar top, which was a sheet of glass laid over a collection of memorabilia, when a familiar silver-blonde head popped up from behind the counter like a jack-in-the-box. The beautiful young shifter leaned on one elbow and looked them over intently, her gaze lingering on Mandy before she turned toward Justin.

"Look who just dropped into my gin joint. A bear I haven't seen in a couple months, and another familiar face who's got trouble written all over her." Nadia set two menus in front of him and Mandy, then in a whirlwind of motion, she spun away. She expertly picked up a loaded tray from the narrow window behind her and lifted it overhead.

She was out from behind the bar area and headed to the nearest table like a brightly coloured hurricane.

The group of burly men she approached had been getting louder and louder, shouted complaints giving way to swinging arms and outright snarling. But with Nadia's arrival, instead of being one second away from what seemed to be bloodshed, they all shot to their feet. They waited politely in silence for the petite blonde to put down their food before resettling into their chairs, their loud conversation now controlled as she twirled away to talk to other customers.

He didn't realize he'd been staring until he felt a tug on his sleeve, and turned back to see Mandy watching Nadia's progress through the bar with equal fascination.

"What kind of shifter is she, and why does she look familiar?"

"Nadia is a lynx. She was in Whitehorse during the bear conclave—at the swimming pool, if you remember."

"Oh." Her face twisted at the unhappy memories the mention of that day must have brought back. "I think I saw her, but that whole day is a bit of a blur."

"Makes sense. There was lot going on at that time." He thought back a little harder. It was no wonder the lynx wasn't instantly recognizable—Mandy had been quickly ensconced in the Takhini pack house while her abusive ex-husband was being dealt with. "Don't worry, she won't be offended you don't remember her."

Nadia moved decisively through the room for a moment before Mandy spoke again. "She's good at her job."

"She is," Justin agreed. "She owns the place, and it's pretty much *the* place in town. Although she has a few advantages not all of us enjoy."

Mandy waited expectantly, but Justin shook his head. "I'll explain, but we should eat first," he insisted.

Another waitress took their order, and their food arrived in quick order. The entire time they ate, Mandy's gaze kept darting around the room, following Nadia.

He expected her to demand an answer far sooner than she actually did, turning to him as if she'd partially solved a mystery.

"There's something more to the story, isn't there? Other than she owns this bar."

"What makes you say that?"

Mandy pointed around the room at different groups of diners. "Bear. Wolf. Wolverine. Fox. And at least three other shifters I can't identify without getting closer. But there's no growling or posturing going on. In fact, the oddest thing is they're all acting as if they actually *like* each other, not that they're barely holding it together."

He was pretty damn proud that she'd figured it out. "Smart lady. Nadia's an Omega. A special one."

That was enough for the moment as he paid the bill then guided Mandy toward the door. She was still distracted, staring over her shoulder at the lynx as they left.

Her expression said she was thinking hard, so Justin remained extra alert as he headed them toward their destination. His heart leapt when she slipped her fingers around his arm and snuggled up against him as if she belonged there.

Which she totally did...as far as he was concerned.

Finally even his pleasure at her unconscious act was overruled as his curiosity got the better of him. "What's on your mind, darling?"

"Nadia. NLT. That's a big place for her to run, and yet you said she's doing well. I'm impressed—she doesn't look as if she's strong enough to handle dealing with hard-headed shifters."

"The size of the person doesn't dictate their skills," Justin pointed out. "I don't judge you by the fact you could fit into my pocket. Also—I told you. She's an Omega. Doesn't take away from her skills in running a profitable business, but it helps stop her clientele from burning it to the ground."

"I didn't see a single lynx in there, so I don't know what good her being an Omega is," Mandy argued.

"For some reason the Omega woo-woo that makes people happy and settle down from their emotional outbursts doesn't just work on her kind, but on all shifters."

Mandy jerked to a complete stop in the middle of the street. "That's not possible. Omegas can only control their own kind."

"Right, it's not possible," he agreed, drawing her with him to the safety of the other side of the street. "Still true, though."

She shook her head. "I've never heard of such a thing, but I guess that explains why she showed up when things got out of control at the bear conclave."

"The wolves arranged it. More specifically, Tyler's wife, if I remember correctly."

A small laugh escaped her. "Caroline?"

"Yup."

Mandy leaned in closer and spoke quietly as if sharing state secrets. "She's one scary human. I mean, I like her, and she was very kind to me, but I'd prefer to get on the bad side of a wolverine shifter before pissing her off."

"You and me, both." Justin tucked a loose strand of hair behind Mandy's ear, desperate to touch her, and using the only small gesture he could right now.

Claim her.

He couldn't even blame the thought on his bear. They both wanted the same thing. Not just her body, but all of her, and the thought increased his impatience even while reminding him why they had to go slow.

I set the speed, she'd said.

The moment stretched between them, Mandy's smile softening as her gaze drifted over him. He could swear he saw hunger in her eyes, and he was about to burst out and say something inappropriate when she pulled back.

She widened her stance and planted her fists on her hips, becoming all fiery and indignant.

"I'll have you know I'm not *that* tiny." She huffed and drew herself to her full height, which meant he was looking down at the top of her head. "Fit into your pocket, *ha.*"

"Oh, I'm sorry. I stand corrected. You're a veritable Amazon."

"Damn, right." Mandy grinned, then took his hand and marched boldly at his side. "And don't you forget it."

"I won't."

Justin stopped them outside their destination, Wolf Brothers Wild Adventures, opening the door and gesturing her in.

He paused before following her. He took a final glance up and down the street, uncertain what had caused him to hesitate, but nothing seemed out of place. A few people wandered on the boardwalk, but everything was quiet, and he stepped slowly into the shop, the sense of foreboding like a lingering cloud of mist. Uncertain and unclear.

7

———

oy and frustration whirled in Mandy's gut.

Justin had been nothing but carefully attentive, giving her the space that she'd demanded. She had nothing at all to complain about in his behavior.

So why did she feel all tangled up inside?

Some of her confusion made sense. She hadn't come to any answers regarding her family situation. Her email remained unanswered, and until her family on the island made contact, her hands were tied. And someone out there had broken into her home, and she still didn't know who.

But the good things were *good*—and as she peeked around the outdoor-equipment shop, a warm thrill of anticipation shoved all her concerns aside.

The wolf shifter who greeted them was a handsome man with dark hair and a layer of scruff on his chin. "Hi. I'm Caden—I've been waiting for you. Everything is laid out. Safety helmet, winter gear. If you need any different sizes we've got them in the back. Come with me."

Justin nodded his approval, grabbing both their piles of

supplies off the counter and following her into the back room where a row of lockers stood for them to store their belongings. On the opposite wall they'd opened the shop doors, two huge garage doors letting in the cool air and offering an amazing view of the scenery.

Mandy slipped on the snowsuit, but her gaze kept returning to the horizon. It was impossible to stop smiling. "I take it we're going out on that beautiful snowy ridge."

"There's plenty of time before sunset. Caden here is going to be our guide. He and his brother Cole are a couple of the best backcountry men I know," Justin offered.

"Compliment willingly accepted," Caden teased. "I'm still charging you full price. Your boss can afford it."

Justin made a rude noise. "My boss owns your ass, and you know it."

"Nothing of the kind." The proclamation spouted from an identical face to Caden's as the second wolf entered the room. "Caden's *mate* owns his ass. The rest of us just borrow it so we can kick it every now and then."

The brothers pounded each other on the shoulders good-naturedly before turning to help Justin and Mandy pull on the rest of their winter gear.

When all four of them were dressed, they marched into the yard behind the shop where row upon row of skidoos were lined up. Three machines had been brought forward for them to use, two large and one smaller. Although using those words to describe the sleds were understatements—*ginormous* and *extra-large* were probably more accurate.

Now that they were actually there, Mandy felt a stir of anxiety at what she was about to attempt.

Caden leaned down to look her in the eye. "What's wrong?"

She answered honestly. "I like the idea of sledding, but I'm going to guess these are pretty powerful machines."

It was too hard to admit she wasn't confident she'd be able to control them. Struck too close to Justin's comment about her being tiny.

Only Caden patted her on the shoulder. "You can control big, powerful beasts better than you know."

A snicker escaped in the background, and she glanced to her right to see Justin glaring at Cole. She turned her face away quickly, hiding her smile before Justin could see.

Caden explained where to find the controls, Mandy nodding as she laid her hands on the grips and tried to commit it to memory. "Excuse me if I drive like a two-year-old."

"Nah, you'll do great. We've got a special training method, as long as you and Justin are okay with it." The wolf turned to the bear who had just settled onto one of the oversized sleds. "I know you guys don't do mates and such, but I don't want to get on the wrong side of a pissed-off bear. Are you okay if I ride along with Mandy for the first while to show her the ropes?"

Justin's forehead furled instantly, then his gaze darted back and forth between the wolf and Mandy before he spoke. "Up to Mandy."

A skip of satisfaction warmed her inside. That wasn't what he had wanted to say—she knew that—but it was the right answer.

It was also silly. She turned to face the wolf, raising a brow. "Considering your mate would rip your ears off if you did anything untoward, of course I'm okay with it."

Cole snickered again. Justin looked uncomfortable for a moment as if he'd just realized how foolish his magnanimous gesture was.

With a laugh Caden was behind her, his lithe wolf body tucked against her as he placed his hands on top of hers on the controls. "Well played, my lady," he murmured. "Let's get you comfortable driving, shall we?"

She moved her hands with his as he reminded her of the commands quietly a second before making the motion. Instantly they were out the gate and shooting up the snowy road to a trail behind the shop that led to the outskirts of town and into the wilderness.

At the beginning, Mandy had to concentrate so hard on driving she was barely aware of their surroundings. She was barely aware of *anything* but the controls, and Caden's continued instruction.

Slowly, though, other sensations broke through. The cool air turned to cold as the sled moved quicker, a rush of current against her cheeks like a winter day's wind. The sunshine on her shoulders fought valiantly to offer a cloak of warmth, but the changing seasons were more advanced here in the north than they'd been in Whitehorse. The brilliant light was pretty but a feeble opponent against the encroaching chill.

She was feeling more confident by the time Caden directed her to bring them to a stop at a lookout point above the town. The neatly laid-out streets were bright-coloured dashes against the white surroundings, the Top of the World Highway stretching like a ribbon from north to south.

Caden stopped the motor. The sudden quiet as the others joined them left her ears echoing for a second before they adjusted to the quieter sounds of nature. In the wilderness there were always living, moving things.

Even the wind was alive as they stood and soaked it all in for a moment.

Suddenly Cole was stripping down. "Sorry, guys, but I need a little time in my fur. You're welcome to join me, or I'll just run alongside the rest of you from here on."

Mandy was tempted, but she wasn't sure what the protocol was. She glanced up to Justin to see what he thought.

He shrugged. "Let's go for it. Two of us, two wolves. Pretty sure we can outrun their asses."

Caden stuck out his tongue while he ditched his clothing into the bag on the back of his sled. "You have some sort of fascination with my ass," he drawled. "I don't think that's healthy."

Mandy hid her amusement. Out of consideration for Justin's possessive instincts, she turned her back on the others so she could quickly get naked and shift to her fur.

The sensation was amazing, as always, as she changed to the one part of her nature that she'd never fought against or argued with. Her bear was *her* while being something more. More in touch with her surroundings, more willing to take control.

What had been a cool wind a moment earlier was now balmy, and she stretched, catlike, taking a deep breath and lifting her face to the sun.

Justin had shifted as well, an enormous grizzly on the extreme end of the *big* spectrum as much as she was on the far side of *small*. He plopped in front of her, resting his chin on his paws and offering a bearish grunt.

"Whoa, you're...*you*. Wow." Caden paused, bare feet planted in the snow beside her. He seemed to forget he was naked as he remained in human form and stared at Mandy. "I had no idea. Excuse me while I fall all over myself. I've never seen a shifter like you before."

Justin rolled over just far enough to bump Caden in the ankles and send him sprawling to the ground.

The man laughed good-naturedly. "Okay, okay. I'll stop ogling, but that doesn't mean I'm not impressed."

Discomfort slipped in for a moment, and once again she turned her focus to Justin, hoping for a clue of how to deal with Caden's unexpected admiration.

He'd rolled to his back and was scratching on the ground happily, totally uncaring about the dignity of his position.

Perfect. Mandy followed his example, rolling to the ground and giving herself a firm squirm against the hard-packed snow. The sensation was delicious, and she gave an extra wiggle.

She only felt a little guilty that she hadn't timed her roll very well when she knocked into Caden's feet, and the wolf ended up on his back again.

He lifted a hand in the air. "Enough, you two. I give up,"

He shifted on the spot, he and his brother changing into large Arctic wolves, black fur with white markings, Caden with a black muzzle, Cole's white.

The four of them exchanged a glance before Cole threw back his head and let loose a howl of happiness. Like a starter gun going off, his cry triggered motion, Caden breaking to the right, Mandy following Justin to the left.

They ran. The snow under their feet shook, echoing with low thumps as they moved over the hills wind-like, drifting in one direction before following the contours of the land in another until Mandy's blood was pumping, and she felt more alive than she had for a long time.

They stopped often, just for a few seconds to look into the

next valley or back over the town. It was wonderful and exciting, and she never wanted to stop running, even as she was eager to get back to the snowmobile to try to drive it all over.

The new experience was like a drug on her senses, joy rising that she was there. That Justin was there, and that together they were free to enjoy.

The sky lit up with the colours of sunset as the shortening day of the northern hemisphere slipped toward night. The sun sank slowly behind the western range, fingers of red and gold painting the hills with streaks from the brush of a wild artist.

She noticed another couple of sleds leaving town, following their recent tracks up the mountains. Probably more customers, although it seemed a little late to just be starting out. She didn't think anything more of it until the wolves took off without another word, racing away and leaving her and Justin behind.

She looked again, and this time a touch of fear rose as she realized the new sleds were on a path that would lead them straight to where she and Justin stood.

Communication while in bear form was a lot more basic, but Justin made it plain something was wrong as he turned to her, crowding her in a move that was clearly protective. He pushed her toward the new tracks left by the wolves—ignoring their earlier meanderings, Caden and Cole had taken a beeline path back to the snowmobiles, the route sending them sliding down a steep hill for the last part of the journey.

Mandy paused at the edge and looked down, caution stilling her feet. At the bottom of the hill, the wolves had shifted, leaping on the sleds, engines roaring as they spun to pursue the intruders without bothering to get dressed.

That was all she had time to see before Justin caught

her from behind, looping his arms around her then launching into the air. Her breath stuck in her throat.

He twisted in mid-air to land on his back with her paws resting on his shoulders, using him like a giant furry sled. Faster and faster they went, snow flying up in wide waves on either side of them.

Something was wrong—that was clear—but she wasn't worried. She should have been, but the trip was far too exhilarating and exciting, and she trusted implicitly that Justin would get them back to safety.

They hadn't even slid to a stop at the bottom of the hill when Justin shifted. She followed his lead, changing to human as he spoke.

"We're taking my sled. Pull on your things then stay with me. We'll let Caden and Cole take care of our visitors."

They sprinted across the short distance to where her things rested on the ground. Cole must have shoved them off the seat where she'd left them before he'd raced off. Mandy jerked on her clothes as quickly as possible, but she was still the last one ready, swinging a leg over the back of the sled and wrapping her hands around Justin's waist. The buzz of the wolves' engines was already fading, the sleds disappearing over a distant rise as they moved in hot pursuit of the intruders.

"Hold on tight," Justin ordered a split second before they were off in a cloud of snow.

⁓

STUPID. *Stupid bloody idiot.*

It was completely and totally stupid for him to have dropped his guard like that, and Justin mentally kicked his own ass the entire trip back into town.

Even though the wolves were chasing their mysterious followers into the wilderness, Justin wasn't going to take any more chances. Instead of returning directly to the shop yard, he took a different route, roaring down back alleys in a twisted path until he reached the underground parking for the safe house. He triggered the master switch on his keychain, and the door opened instantly, allowing him to drive straight in. A moment later he had everything shut down, Mandy hurrying at his side toward the stairs.

Not until they were back in the apartment with the security system armed did he begin to relax. Their little adventure had not turned out like he'd expected. So much for a relaxing snow day.

"We're safe now." Justin guided her down the hallway to the bathroom. "Strip," he ordered. "I'll be right back.

He raced to the kitchen and filled the kettle, plugging it in and setting it to turn off automatically once it was heated. He hurried back to make sure Mandy had crawled into a steaming-hot shower.

He rounded the corner to discover her standing there, fingers trembling as she held her wet shirt away from her body.

She glanced up, dark eyes like deep wells as she met his gaze. "I'm sorry, it appears I must've gotten the zipper on my pants stuck. We were in such a hurry, and now I can't make it budge, and..."

Her teeth chattered so hard he couldn't understand the next part of what she said.

Justin dropped to his knees, jiggling the zipper to try and free it from where the fabric was caught between the metal teeth, but it was no use. "You've jammed this beyond repair. Congratulations."

"G-g-go me," Mandy chattered.

Justin lifted the edge of her shirt, carrying it over her head so she was naked from the waist up. "Give me a second, and I'll get you free."

He caught hold of either side of her zipper. One hard jerk broke it completely, then he pulled the wet fabric away from her, peeling it down to leave her standing naked before him.

Tempting, tasty skin that he wanted nothing more than to experience all over again.

He was still on his knees before her, and she took a two-handed grip on the front of his shirt. "Oh, look. It seems I'm naked, and you're going to be too," Mandy warned him.

She didn't give him time to protest. As if he would have —he wasn't a stupid bear about everything.

Mandy jerked her hands apart and his buttons flew. She ripped the fabric down his shoulders and off his arms before the little plastic pieces had finished rattling on the floor.

They stood at the same moment. Mandy was already working his pants, and it didn't matter that her hands were cold, they were heaven against his skin.

But when she wrapped her fingers around his rising erection, Justin swore.

"Your hands are like ice," he complained.

She pulled another rush of pleasure/pain from him as she stroked firmly a couple of times. "I know they're cold. That's why I need to warm them on the hottest thing around." Mandy hummed happily, staring down at her fingers with a sultry smile curling her lips. "I don't know that I've ever seen a two-handed warmer before."

Justin was still laughing when he picked her up and brought them together under the shower, the hot water insanely good after the intense cold on the sled. It made his skin tingle everywhere, but it was Mandy's touch that flashed the hottest as her soapy hands worked up a lather over him.

"This isn't right," he complained. "You don't need to do all the work."

Mandy twisted in front of him, full curves drawing him like a sexual beacon.

She grabbed another bar of soap and opened it for him, pressing it into his hands. "Here. I don't want you to feel left out."

Justin was in heaven. Soft curves dipped and rose under his touch. He ran his hands over her, the sweet-scented soap making friction disappear, but the heat and erotic sensations remained.

She kept on touching him as well. And as fast as his heart had been pumping that afternoon, it had nothing on the race in his chest right now. She curled her fingertips around his erection again, stroking for a moment before her hands slid away, over his hipbones and along the muscles of his torso.

"I think Chicken is a very nice town, but if we need to move again, I propose a tropical island, please."

Justin laughed, even as he let his hands continue to play over her curves. "Strange change of topic. Are you tired of the cold?"

She shook her head. "Oh, it's plenty warm here, but if we go somewhere tropical, maybe we can find a *clothing optional* location. I could handle looking at you all day long."

So picky, but unless it was a private beach, that meant others would be able to see her too, and he really wasn't very fond of that idea. "Tropical island. You need to add that to your list."

Her eyes lit up. "Oh yes. Speaking of my list..."

Justin held back a shout as she fell to her knees. He attempted to catch her, but she slipped through his fingers. She hadn't fallen. It'd been deliberate, and a second later, understanding hit. What she intended to do. Staring up at him as she planted her hands on his thighs and offered him a sweet smile.

"You don't need to do that."

Mandy offered him a mock pout. "My choice," she reminded him.

Well, if she put it that way. Who was he to deny her heart's desire?

He was torn between offering a brisk nod or making some smart-ass comment. Something to lighten the mood and keep from making this into something big and momentous.

He opened his mouth, but all that came out was a gurgled moan.

Mandy had skipped any kind of foreplay, going straight to a one-two-punch move. One, grasping him at the base of his cock and tilting him downward before two, opening her mouth and surrounding him.

He'd been in the shower, so he'd been hot and wet, but this—?

Not the same. Not *remotely* the same.

"Holy *fuck*—"

Mandy pulled back, a slight *pop* accompanying the motion. "Yes? Am I doing it right?"

"There is no way to do this wrong," he told her. "Trust me."

Mandy grinned. "Okay, let me rephrase that. Is there a way to do this *better*?"

He brushed his knuckles over her cheek. "Want to be a star pupil, do you?"

"Anything worth doing is worth doing right."

He grinned. Placing his hand over hers, he adjusted the angle. "Squeeze with this hand if you want, up and down. Your fist will give you a way to stop my cock from going too deep. And here." He took her other hand and brushed her finger over the most sensitive part. "Remember this spot. If you use your fingers or your tongue on there, trust me, you'll get the response you're looking for."

"I'll remember that," she promised. "Just do me a favour, and make a lot of noise when I do something you like."

Which is why Justin found himself feeling all sorts of foolish as he willingly followed instructions.

She licked delicately, and he hummed.

She closed her lips around him and sucked, and the hum became a low growl. But when she got her fist going, trying to time each pump with a combination suck and tongue swirl, Justin lost his ever-loving mind and broke out into a full growl.

He slammed his palms against the tiles opposite him, tilting his hips on every move as he offered encouragement.

"Right there. Hard, Mandy, right there..."

It was like having a front-row seat at the most spectacular porn show ever, especially considering he wasn't just watching, but experiencing a Technicolor and sensory overload, with all of the Disney special effects thrown in. If they made a ride like this at one of the theme parks, the developers would be multibillionaires before the end of the first month.

She was looking up at him, lashes fluttering to knock the water off that was lightly misting over her, and he shifted his shoulders to guard her more. The position made her clutch at his butt with one hand, working him with the other, and he could have sworn the decorations in the bathroom changed from blues and whites into swirling doodads and purple comets shooting into the sky.

"Coming," he warned, but she just made a sound of affirmation and then stilled her hand while she did that tongue/sucking thing again.

The comets exploded. Rockets took off, and the entire space program and Fourth of July shot through the end of his cock.

Mandy swallowed hard a couple of times before pulling back, her hand moving over him too gently to help him finish. He covered her fingers with his to jerk out the rest of his response, his seed flying onto her cheek and down her breasts.

Which set him off all over again.

Head spinning, the only thing he was fully aware of was they weren't nearly done. Justin reached for her and prepared to blow her mind.

8

———

Mandy sat back on her heels to take a deep breath and...well, honestly? Gloat.

Forget that she'd knocked off an item on her list, she'd thoroughly enjoyed his response. And to top it off, it seemed in spite of her best efforts, Justin was nowhere near done.

Which, *hello*, lovely side effect of being shifters.

She didn't mind at all when he tucked his hands around her and brought her to her feet. He paused for only a second before lifting her higher and draping her over his body. The shower spray struck her skin with teeny dancing needles of fine, warm mist, the prickles contrasting deliciously with the smooth heat of his tongue as he licked and teased and kissed.

"Can't stop."

The words were growled desperately, and she hurried to reassure him there was no place she'd rather be.

"I'm good right here," she promised.

He seemed pleased with her answer. He nipped at the edge of her breast before following it with a tender kiss. "So beautiful. So damn brave."

Mandy let her happiness escape in a long, contented sigh.

"I've been called beautiful before, but honestly, it means so much more when it's not only about something that's skin deep." She let go of his shoulders, trusting him to hold her in place as she pressed her palms to his face and allowed her contentment to shine through. "Thank you for saying I'm brave."

"Not just words," he offered, rubbing their noses together affectionately. "Everything you do screams how brave you are."

"It hasn't always been that way," she said.

He held her against him, their frantic, passionate rush transforming into something different. "It's always been there for people who knew how to see. You're not just being brave for others anymore. Now you're being brave for you."

Mandy's heart swelled. If she wasn't careful she was going to admit she was falling...

No. She wasn't ready to admit it. "Again, thank you."

She pressed their lips together and kissed him, softly at first then with growing intensity until he was back to making some of those intoxicating noises she'd pulled from him earlier.

Her thought was that he would slow down and take them back into the bedroom, but that idea quickly vanished as he pressed her shoulders against the wall of the shower, their lips connected, her legs wrapped around his sturdy body.

His fingers drifted over her belly and between her legs, and she made a noise of her own as he stroked her sex. Over and over, fingers barely slipping in, then out, then over her clit until she was desperate to be filled.

He adjusted position until the thick head of his cock

pressed into her, and they both made noises as he slid home, satisfaction and delight echoing from the walls of the shower. Her higher tone and his deep accompaniment blended together and swirled in the enclosure. She moaned, and their noises of pleasure mixed together into musical tones that echoed back over her skin in an auditory seduction.

Staccato beats joined the chorus as he withdrew then thrust forward. Over and over, their bodies impacted against each other as the rapid pulse reverberated off the walls.

"Oh, *Justin*—"

Her breathing sped up, fingertips digging into his shoulders as he pulsed his hips against hers, cock driving into her passage and sending her senses reeling. They were both panting. Gasping for air as he rested his forehead on the tiles beside her. His breath hot on her skin.

Somewhere in her past she'd lived a life full of pain and uncertainty. She'd been captive in a way that her shifter soul should never have had to experience, but here and now, all that vanished. Faded into a misty haze that was no longer a part of her life. Or at least, no longer a part of her future.

This was her new life. Pleasure was being bestowed upon her until she was ready to explode with it. No retreat —no escape, but she didn't want a way out.

She *needed*.

With every fiber of her being, she needed—not just the sex, but the caring that was implicit in his every touch.

As if sensing she'd vanished down a rabbit hole of memories and introspection, Justin slowed. His hands on her hips cradled her carefully. He switched from pounding into her as if welding them together to silent, long slow strokes that nearly drew him from her body before connecting them an inch at a time. Finishing with pure, complete one-ness.

Over.

And over.

Pleasure creeping over her like molasses on a winter's day.

Senses tingling.

Her breath caught in her chest as he lifted his gaze to hers and slipped...in...all...the...way.

And stopped.

He pressed their foreheads together. "I have been dreaming about this for fucking ever, excuse the language."

Inside a bubble expanded, reaching up and twisting her lips. Happiness taking her by storm until, in spite of the edge of urgency pulsing between them, in spite of the need she had to finish this together, in spite of his cock buried in her body—

Laughter escaped between one breath and the next.

His eyes widened in the second she was watching him before she caught his face in her hands and pulled their mouths back together. Lips meshing as she tightened her legs, digging her heels into his ass. Squeezing her core around his shaft. Loving the sensation of fullness as he growled into her mouth and shifted position, pressing even deeper.

A half-dozen strokes followed, and another six after that. Each one deliberate, as if he were stroking a bow over the strings of a Stradivarius. Her body reacted, rising rapidly toward completion. Hovering for one second before teetering over the edge and flashing a bright, white ecstasy over her.

Their breaths mingled as he swore, capturing her lips a second later to swallow her moan. The fingers caressing her ass gentled as her sex grabbed his shaft in a final desperate pulse.

Time slipped past as they returned to their senses. The water was still hot as it cascaded over them, but a delicious sense of relaxation and satisfaction had replaced any worry.

And cold?

Vanquished seemingly forever.

Mandy slid her fingers into his hair and tugged lightly to get him to look at her. "So. We had visitors?"

Guilt and dismay arrived far too quickly, furling a line between his brows. "I'm a shitty bodyguard."

She shook her head. "That's not what *my* body is currently saying. It's singing your praises pretty damn hard."

A grin escaped before his expression turned serious again. "We had visitors."

"But we're safe? Here, in the apartment?"

He nodded, although he still looked embarrassed.

She raised a brow. "Then as far as I'm concerned, you were doing your job, although I certainly hope I wasn't just a job to you."

"Hell, no." He spat out the words so fast she had to dip her head to hide her smile.

They untangled themselves, taking turns to slide under the water one last time to rinse. Justin found them towels, and they dried off in companionable silence.

Mandy caught him by the hand and led him into the bedroom, tugging him to the mattress and under the covers before he could protest.

"You said Cole and Caden would track our *visitors*, yes?"

He nodded slowly.

Mandy stretched her arms and let a yawn escape,

smiling again as his gaze lingered on her naked breasts. She curled herself against him and pulled the covers up to their chins. "Then we let them track. I want a nap."

"But I should—"

"—wanna nap with *you*."

Her decisive statement was enough to stop him in his tracks, and suddenly she was surrounded by a hot, naked bear-shifter of extraordinary size.

The sheets were silky soft, his arm under her head was rock solid, but the hand draped over her belly touched her skin with the most delicate of strokes as she let the fears and excitement of the day carry her off into slumber.

JUSTIN LAY WRAPPED around perfection and wondered what the hell he'd been thinking.

He *hadn't* been thinking, or at least not with his big head, from the instant he'd gotten her naked. Or even before—

Yet after her decisive reminder that they were safe, he let his self-flagellating thoughts go and instead savoured the warmth of being tangled with her.

Justin actually fell asleep, waking as she stretched lazily against him, her smooth skin sliding over his then away far too quickly as she rolled from the bed and disappeared into the bathroom.

He dressed then headed to the kitchen to wait for her to reappear.

Mandy joined him only a minute or two later, dressed to go out. "I'm hungry. Want to go back to NLT?" She paused, wrinkling her nose in the most adorable manner. "If you think it's safe."

"Out of all the places we could go, that's one of the safest," he admitted.

She held his hand the entire trip, the tall street lamps brightening their route. He expected her to glance around nervously, but she marched with confidence at his side, asking non-stop questions about his job, and his place in Yellowknife where he lived most of the time, working with Tyler.

Instead of him distracting her from the unknowns of the day, she was in complete control. In fact, whatever magic she was using, during the short walk she managed to get him to spill the beans and share a secret about his boss.

He pulled open the door at NLT as Mandy laughed behind her hand. "And Tyler's never eaten them since?"

Justin shook his head and guided her toward a side booth. "Who knew too many malted milk chocolates could have that effect on a big guy like him?"

He lifted her to the seat, stepping back rapidly as she scowled then swatted at him. "You need to stop throwing me around like a sack of potatoes," she complained.

"I like carrying you." He just grinned harder as he dodged the flimsy napkin she tossed in his direction.

Justin seated himself so he could see the door, back on guard.

It wasn't unexpected. Nadia showed up at their table about thirty seconds after the waitress had taken their order.

She eyed them both. "Troubles, kids?"

"No trouble." Justin stared her down, not willing to admit anything if he didn't have to. Besides, he wasn't *really* lying—there was no trouble currently happening, at that moment, in that location.

Nadia raised a brow but didn't say anything specifically judgmental.

In fact, she turned to Mandy and offered a welcoming smile. "If you're hanging around town for a while, pop in on Thursday night. That's ladies night. And line dancing."

Mandy's eyes lit up. "If someone can teach me—I've never done that before."

"Of course." Nadia caught her by the fingers and squeezed. Then she tossed a stern command at Justin. "Ladies only. Don't even think about trying to sneak in. I'll kick your furry butt out myself if I catch you."

Justin pulled himself up, drawing his dignity around him like a shield. "*If* you catch me is the key word in that statement."

She turned on him, folding her arms over her chest. "Oh, sugar, don't delude yourself."

They held a good-natured staring match for a moment before a huge bear shifter shuffled from the shadows to whisper in Nadia's ear.

She nodded then turned to offer a farewell. "Martin says I'm needed at the bar. I'll see you soon, Mandy. And Justin?" She narrowed her gaze. "Let me know if I can give you a hand."

He dipped his head. He wasn't foolish enough to turn down her help, but hopefully it wouldn't come to that.

They were nearly done with their meal when Caden and Cole marched through the door, hair tousled, clothing askew. The brothers spotted them and headed straight to the table.

"Head's up," Justin warned.

Mandy slid closer and tangled her fingers around his biceps.

The wolves tossed themselves onto the padded bench on the opposite side of the table. They were both breathing hard, and Cole grabbed the water jug and lifted it to his mouth to drink straight from the pitcher.

Justin eyed them before glancing toward the door suspiciously. "Where're your targets, boys?"

"Don't start with us, big guy, or I'll go full-moon on your ass," Cole warned.

"It's a reasonable question." All three of them pivoted to stare at Mandy who'd been the one to speak. She shrugged. "Justin said you were the best trackers around. I'm surprised to see you here, without anyone."

Caden growled as he slammed a hand on the table. Justin had his fingers trapped in an iron-clad fist between one second and the next.

Silence cut like a knife.

Mandy clicked her tongue in warning, and Justin forced himself to let the wolf free.

Caden glared at Justin, but the wolf muttered *sorry* before letting out a gruff grunt. "We did track them. But they hit the edge of the river and swam off, headed north. No freaking way was I getting in the water to chase down a couple of bears in their native territory."

Beside him, Mandy glanced up in confusion. "Swam off?"

Justin grimaced. It was unwelcome news. Out of all the shifter species he'd expected trouble from, their new suspects were not on the list. "He means polar bears."

Caden raised his hands in a shrug. "There's not much use trying to follow them without contacting someone at—"

"You *think* they were polar bears," Cole snapped. "I'm not sure. You got in the way—I couldn't see clearly."

His brother whirled on him and glared. "Don't be a pain in the ass, bro."

"Don't be a jerk, bro," Cole retorted before glancing

across the table. "I'm going to track them down."

Mandy dipped her head, but she held a little tighter to Justin's arm. "But you're sure that they're gone. For now, I mean?"

Caden leaned back, wrinkling his nose. "We did a lap around town before tracking you here. There were only two unfamiliar scents, and they're long gone. I can't tell you how sorry we are they accessed a couple of our sleds like that. Must have hot-wired them."

She blinked in surprise, obviously caught on his earlier comment. "You know everyone in town by their scent?"

Justin leaned down to whisper in her ear. "It's a wolf thing. Be thankful they don't sniff like dogs do."

He secretly patted her butt.

Her eyes widened.

Of course with their abilities, the wolves had heard his comment. The brothers growled a warning, but his tease had brought back a flicker of a smile to Mandy's lips, and that's all that mattered.

She offered him a quick wink before facing the brothers again. "But you can track them?"

Caden jerked a thumb at his brother. "I couldn't, but I bet he can. Pain in the ass."

"Jerk." Cole dipped his head. "I came back to make sure you guys were okay, but I'm heading out again. I swear I'll find them. There's something..."

The wolf looked off into the distance, his eyes going out of focus as if he were concentrating on something only he could see. More weird wolf mumbo-jumbo, Justin figured, but the offer of tracking was a good one. It would allow him to stay in Chicken and protect Mandy, and still get to the bottom of the mystery.

"Thanks for that," Justin said with sincerity.

Mandy reached across the table and squeezed Cole's hand. "Yes, thank you."

Caden slapped his brother on the shoulder then motioned toward the door. "Come on, my mate will be waiting. We'll feed you before you take off."

The brothers slipped away, vanishing like shadows.

The next second Nadia stood there again, a beacon of silvery-white. She wore an expression that spoke volumes.

Justin couldn't resist temptation. "Yes? Can I help you?"

Nadia rolled her eyes. "You just can't spit the words out, can you?"

"I have no idea what you're talking about."

"That's fine. You don't have to say anything." The lynx leaned her elbows on the table, speaking directly to Mandy. "I've got your back, sister. I know this one"—she jerked her thumb toward Justin—"will take good care of you. He's a good egg, but just to be sure, I'm calling in favours from all my people. No one gets in or out of Chicken without us knowing. You can relax until Cole gets back. You have my word."

It was the best of all possible promises. Nadia's connections throughout town meant she really did have eyes everywhere.

Justin held out a hand. "You're a good egg too."

Nadia shook his hand firmly. "Don't be modest. You know damn well this is why you brought her here in the first place."

There was no use lying. "Busted."

She stepped back, dipping her head to Mandy before pulling herself up to her full height of a scant five feet. She stuck out her tongue at Justin, then twirled on the spot and marched away, the giant bear who always shadowed her following behind after offering Justin a quick wink.

9

———

There was no good reason to leave town. Not with Cole out on the hunt and the entire town on alert, so Justin reluctantly hunkered down for the count with Mandy.

Or at least that's the story he told his boss when Tyler phoned a few days later.

"...so you see, we're in pretty much the most protected place right here, and we've got all the backup we need."

The bear on the other end of the line was silent for a moment before a soft chuckle carried over the line.

"You're lucky all of this makes sense," Tyler told him. "Because I know damn well you're not suffering, holed up in some godforsaken uncomfortable bug-out house. You're probably in the lap of luxury, aren't you?"

Justin let his gaze meander lazily over Mandy who sat in the recliner opposite him wearing nothing but a sheer nightgown as she glanced through a magazine. "It's pretty rustic," Justin insisted. "It took nearly three days to get lobsters flown in."

Tyler made off-key violin noises on the other end of the

line before turning more serious. "You know I trust you, and you know I want the best for you. Take your time. I've got the goon squad on my back, so I'm nearly as safe as if you were with me."

It wasn't Tyler he was worried about. "And Caroline? Because if you need me, I could always bring Mandy along."

"Now I know you haven't been getting enough sleep. Number one, what kind of monster do you think I am? I took the patrol off Caroline a day after you assigned them. She's a one-man-guerrilla-force all on her own, and she was getting in their way."

Justin laughed. "What's number two?"

Head honcho of all the northern hemisphere bears offered him a cheeky chuckle. "It's awfully hard to woo a woman when you're acting as my bodyguard."

To which Justin didn't even answer, because his boss was right *and* Mandy was right there. He wasn't going to draw any attention to said wooing.

He got off the phone and deliberately crossed the room. It was the work of a moment to pick her up and resettle, this time with her in his lap.

She smiled patiently at him when he tugged the magazine from her fingers and dropped it to the floor. "Tyler and Caroline doing well, I take it?"

"They are. They're back in Yellowknife."

Her expression went guarded. "Oh."

"You're too easy to read," he warned her before caressing a finger down her cheek. "I don't need to go back to work yet. Not until we figure out what's going on with your mysterious strangers."

She nodded slowly. "Tyler is a good boss to be so understanding."

"He's a good friend, first and foremost." Justin dropped a kiss on her nose. "That's what good friends do—they understand what you need, sometimes before you know it yourself."

Mandy wiggled into a more comfortable position, one that brought her warmth into direct contact with the entire front of his torso. She draped her hands over his shoulders, stroking her fingers through his hair as she gazed into his face. "I'm glad you have a friend like that."

She spoke so softly he nearly missed it. The tone of sadness underbrushing her words.

Justin cupped her face in his hands. "You have a friend like that too, you know."

Her lips curved upward. "I have more friends now than before, yes. Caroline and Amy. And now Nadia—she's so sweet to me every time we get together." Mandy frowned. "Do you know why she's sad?"

"Is Nadia sad?" Justin thought back over the week they'd been hanging out in Chicken. "I never noticed."

"Hmmm, maybe I'm wrong." Mandy tugged her fingers through his hair again, still thoughtful.

"Have you heard from your family yet?"

She'd finally told him she'd been waiting to make contact until there was no possible way Todd could interfere in her life.

"Nothing yet, but Internet on the island is pretty caveman-era." Mandy shook her head. "I'm conflicted about what I want. It's been so long since I left that I'd barely know my little sisters, or Nana, or the bears of the island, anymore. My parents were gone years before. Maybe I should just leave it alone, and then I feel guilty for not—"

She slammed her lips close.

"No guilt," he reminded her. "You are an amazing

woman, and whatever happens in the future, I know you're smart enough to make the right decisions."

He tweaked her nose, and she nipped playfully at his fingers. "You're pretty amazing yourself."

His mind turned to another issue. "By the way, you missed naming one of your friends."

She blinked hard before smiling. "So I did."

Justin accepted the kiss she gave him in apology. And the next. And the one after that—well, that one he enjoyed as he took to his feet and carried her blindly down the hall to the bedroom.

He settled them on the bed, cuddling for a while as she murmured happy words around more kisses. Clothes fell away until they were skin on skin. Their touches started soft and teasing before passion flared, and they came together in a bright burst of sensation that made his heart pump and his hopes rise.

This was exactly what he wanted for her. For them. But he wasn't going to push her to make any long-term decisions yet, even though he knew exactly what he wanted.

Her—forever.

A couple mornings later Mandy was standing at the sink beside him, drying the dishes as he finished hand-washing them after breakfast.

"I thought we could go tobogganing today," Mandy suggested. "And then the theater society is showing some golden oldies. You want to go?"

Justin hesitated. "Is it on your list?"

She shook her head.

He thought about it for moment "Aww, what the heck. Not everything has to come off the list."

It was about the longest vacation Justin had taken since high school when he and his friend had begun their climb to the top in the business world, not to mention the bear's political structure. Afternoon naps, late-night dinners, long conversations as they walked everywhere around Chicken.

It really was about the best thing he could imagine, and watching Mandy blossom before his eyes made it even better.

She didn't venture out without him—they were still being cautious, but when they went, she led and he followed, pausing whenever she wanted to chat with the people they had gotten to know in the community.

It was too perfect to last.

His phone rang, and Caden's growly voice greeted him the instant he said *hello*.

"Cole is back, and you're not going to believe this."

"Did he catch them?"

"One of them. Get down here. It'll be easier to explain once you see it."

Caden hung up the phone, leaving Justin wondering.

Mandy wrapped herself around him from the back and pressed a kiss to his biceps. "Who was that?"

"Cole is back."

She stiffened. "And?"

She had the right to know, and it wasn't protecting her to not share the information. "He caught one."

Mandy pulled herself in front of him, eyes going wide before her expression changed into one of sheer determination. "What are we waiting for? Let's go."

What was he waiting for? He didn't want this to end.

Justin pulled himself together before he admitted that and forced her hand.

"What if it's a setup?" he asked instead, voicing his other concerns. "What if there are more of them out there?

What if they're just trying to get you in the same room as one of them for some reason before they do...something?"

Her lips twitched. "There were a lot of *ifs* and *somethings* in that sentence, Justin. Remember our deal? I trust you to keep me safe. If I need to stay here because you're absolutely sure that's the only way, I'll do it. But if I'm safe at your side, we should go."

Yeah he wasn't about to lie, and she was right.

Dammit. She was right. She *was* safe at his side. That's what he needed to convince her of, for now and the future. And there was only one way to face the challenge, and that was to deal with whatever in her past was haunting her, once and for all.

"Grab your stuff, and let's go."

Oh boy, she'd become the best bluffer in town.

Mandy *wanted* to face whoever it was who'd been stalking her, but it was an outright lie to say she was comfortable with the idea.

Nightmares of her days married to Todd kept intruding, but she forced the memories aside by focusing on the big, gentle giant at her side. The wall of protection that he offered.

Nothing would happen to her with Justin around, and so the only thing to be afraid of was backing down.

Justin squeezed her fingers as they stood outside the door of the Wolf Brothers Wild Adventures shop, waiting for her to work up her courage.

The door opened and Caden stepped out, tugging the door closed behind him as he glanced between them. "Take a deep breath and relax," he ordered. "Nadia's here."

Tension drained out of Mandy like pulling a plug from the sink, and she noticed Justin breathed a sigh of relief as well. "Oh, brilliant idea."

"It's always good to have backup in place." Caden grinned before elbowing Justin in the side. "Pulled one over on you, hey, Baloo? You forgot we got the rooten-tootenest cowboy sheriff around in these parts."

Justin made a gagging noise. "I'll be sure to tell her you said so. In those exact words."

Caden's expression twisted slightly. "Aww, you don't have to do that. Seeing as we're kinda busy right now, and all."

"Don't feel like explaining yourself to her, do you?"

The wolf shook his head. "Hell, no. I like my fur on the outside, and my tail knotless, thanks."

They walked through the door, and that eerie sense of calm hit. The one that filled a room when Nadia was trying to keep things under control. Fresh and clean, invigorating and yet slightly drowsy, the scent after a spring rain. Mandy curled her fingers around Justin's hand to tug him forward with her.

There was a lot to take in at one glance. Nadia stood to the left, leaning on the wall. On the opposite side of the room, Cole sat at the table with his fingers wrapped around the frail wrist of a dark-haired young woman...

Mandy's heart leapt with excitement, and she dropped her hold on Justin and sprinted across the room.

~

It all happened in an instant.

Justin's gaze landed on Cole, sitting at a table with his fingers wrapped tightly around the arm of a dark-haired woman. Justin took a closer look, confused for moment until he realized why the stranger looked so familiar. That's when Mandy took off from his side, rushing forward with her hands thrown out in greeting.

"Danielle?"

The next moments passed in a rush of noise and confusion as Mandy pulled the other woman into her arms. Cole stood, and Justin hovered behind Mandy, having chased after her as quickly as he could.

"Oh, Mandy. It *is* you." The other woman burst into tears.

Justin stood at Mandy's back in case he was needed, but it seemed she knew who the other woman was, so he turned to taunt Cole. "Took you long enough."

"There were complications," Cole snapped, all joking aside as he watched Danielle closely.

Obsessively.

Oh shit, that didn't bode well.

Someone cleared their throat loudly, drawing their attention across the room to where Nadia was holding up the wall. She rolled her eyes. "You mustn't think much of me with the way you're both hovering over those women," Nadia complained. "Sit down, all of you. The sooner we figure out this mess, the better."

Mandy refused to let go of Danielle's hand, pulling her into the chair Cole had abandoned, and forcing the men to take positions behind them.

"So she really does know you?" Cole demanded.

Mandy nodded, touching Danielle's face gently. "Although I didn't recognize you for a moment. You've changed."

"Grown up."

Mandy twisted in her chair to offer Justin a brilliant

smile. "Danielle is my middle sister. I haven't seen her or Susanna since I moved away."

Some of his fears faded, but he still had concerns. "But who was with her? Why did she chase us with the snowmobiles? And what was she doing in your apartment?"

Danielle didn't flinch, but she only answered part of his questions. "Trying to get information. We heard rumors, but no one would tell us anything for sure, so I figured I had to find out for myself." Danielle looked Justin up and down slowly, assessing and apparently finding him wanting. "I wanted to know that she was free of the controlling bastard who'd taken her from us."

"I am," Mandy assured her. "Everything has changed, and it's all going to be okay. Justin's boss is the new head of the bear clans, and he's making changes. *Good* changes."

Danielle and Justin exchanged another glance. Her youth was now a lot more apparent after he'd spent some time watching her. She had to be barely out of her teens.

She shrugged then ignored Justin and focused on Mandy, joining their hands. "We'll see. But now that I found you, I want you to come home with me."

"*No.*"

The word jerked out of Justin involuntarily, and the only thing that made it better, *maybe*, was that he wasn't alone in declaring it.

Cole had snapped the word at the same moment, staring at Danielle.

The two women at the table moved as if in a well-choreographed routine. They pushed their chairs back and turned, folding their arms over their chests as they offered stern glares at the men.

"*No?*" Mandy asked in shock.

Justin struggled to find a way to reverse his outburst, but

it was impossible to turn off his protective instincts. "Not until we find out more," he insisted.

"She's my *sister*."

"Which means you trust her," Justin answered back. "Which is exactly what someone with more nefarious purposes like your ex would do. They'd think nothing of using your sister to get at you."

Cole turned on him, pulling his lips back to show teeth. "Are you saying Danielle's bait in a trap?"

The wolf's hackles were up, and Justin motioned for him to relax. "I'm saying we don't do anything without thinking this through."

Dead silence fell at the table. Mandy's gaze burned into him as she made her disapproval clear.

It took Nadia stepping forward to bring them back where the tension was low enough they could think again. The small blonde tugged out a chair and sat in it backward, leaning her arms along the backrest. "Nothing has to be decided this instant," she pointed out.

"I'm not letting Danielle out of my sight," Cole insisted.

"I know, because she was talented enough to give you the slip for such a long time." Nadia clicked her tongue soothingly. "I'm sure she won't be so mean to you, ever again. Poor wittle wolfie."

Cole sputtered even as Danielle's lips twisted into a smirk.

"We can figure out something that keeps everyone around and happy until Mandy has made a decision. Because, unless I'm wrong, and I don't think so, this is *her* decision to make." Nadia pointed at Mandy.

Mandy stood, pulling Danielle into her arms and hugging her tight. "Yes, it is my decision, but there's no way

I can make it unless I have time to talk with my sister. Alone."

She twisted rapidly, fists going to her hips as she glared at both Cole and Justin. "Stop with the growling, guys. If you're worried about Danielle magically whisking me off under your nose"—she shifted her gaze to Justin, her chin tilting up defiantly—"or if you don't trust me to stay around like I promised I would, we'll just sit *here* and talk. But you two have to sit over *there*."

She pointed across the room.

"Cole will be able to hear you," Justin reminded her reluctantly.

The wolf jabbed his fingers into Justin's ribcage like a knife.

Justin didn't care. Mandy's stern expression had softened at his words. She laid a hand on his arm. "I know he can hear. That's not the point. I'm not trying to keep secrets, I just want to be with her, alone."

He nodded, then stepped back as Nadia linked her hands around his arm and Cole's, hauling them toward the door. "See, Cole? See how much easier things go if you just listen to the smarter people in the room?"

Cole snapped his teeth at her, and she laughed.

"Okay, that one was a little mean of me. Come on, Mr. Growly. Your new friend will be here when you get back. I need you to come give me a hand for a minute."

"But she said—"

"Mandy might not mind your bionic wolf hearing, but they deserve privacy. And I really do need your help. Please?" Nadia wheedled.

Cole refused to budge until he got Danielle's attention, speaking softly but most definitely an order. "Don't even *think* about leaving town without me."

Danielle scratched her cheek with her middle finger before turning her attention back to her sister.

Justin was pacified by the fact Mandy seemed completely in control, and comfortable, so he went outside, the doors closing with a solid click behind him.

~

AFTER THE ADRENALINE rush of the last few moments, Mandy was happy to sit back down, catching hold of Danielle's hand again and squeezing it tightly.

"Tell me everything that's happening at home. No, wait. Tell me how you found me. No, wait..." Mandy shook her head. "I feel as if we've got forever to catch up on, and I don't even know what to ask you."

Daniel glanced toward the door "Then don't. Let me ask the questions instead. Are you really okay? We'd heard terrible things, but it's still nearly impossible to get any up-to-date news on the island."

"I really am good. I'm free," she told her sister, honest relief in her voice.

Danielle didn't jump up and down with excitement the way Mandy had hoped she would.

Instead her sister took another glance at the door. "Who's he? The big bear? Because he doesn't look any safer then Todd."

Oh. Now Mandy understood why the private discussion. "Justin is nothing at all like Todd. Okay, yes, he's a big, possessive bear, but in all the ways that count, they're nothing alike. He's been so careful with me."

"He hauled you halfway across the north on a moment's notice."

Mandy gave her sister a warning glance. "He brought

me to Chicken to protect me because *you* and someone else broke into my apartment, and we were afraid it was someone associated with Todd."

Daniel relaxed the tiniest bit. "That was me and one of the clan. Susanna wanted to come, but she's a lousy tracker. And I couldn't take any chances. Even now, what if you're just saying something because you think it's what's best for us? For the family? That's what you did before."

Her past was coming back to haunt her. "Not the same thing at all," Mandy's insisted. "Todd is out of my life for good."

"Then come to the island. We need you there. We need you to make a difference."

"I've been gone for eight years. The island isn't home anymore," Mandy protested.

Silence hung in the air. Her sister seemed to deflate, slouching back in her chair.

"Okay, this is going to sound stupid, but you're like the big sister in a storybook who's been shut away in an ivory tower for years." Danielle made a face. "I know about you, and I care for you, but I...don't *know* you as my sister."

"*Yet*," Mandy added, her own sorrow adding to the mix. "But I understand what you mean. I want the best for you, and Susanna, and the rest of the island, but you're all distant memories, in a way."

They stared at each other sadly. "Tough truths, hey, sis?"

"The toughest," Mandy agreed.

Danielle's expression grew softer. "Here's another tough truth. I'm sorry, but Nana passed away a couple of weeks ago. That's when we started looking for you."

Mandy had expected this to happen at some point. She'd been away for so long, and she'd somehow known that her grandmother would be gone before they could reconnect. Their relationship was...*difficult* to say the least. The cold spot that had formed inside her when she chose to leave all those years ago and her Nana hadn't protested—that coldness protected her now, and made her numb to grief.

She went with polite, although she didn't really remember her Nana very fondly. "I'm sorry I wasn't there."

"She knew you'd done your best for the family, but now that you're no longer with Todd, that means you need to return," Danielle insisted. "It's your responsibility. You're the oldest. You're supposed to take over leadership."

Awkwardness turned into discomfort as all the things she'd missed doing over the years once again slid from her grasp. Mandy shook her head. "Not necessarily. I gave up the right to rule the island when I left. That should put you next in line. Why don't *you* take the position?"

Danielle let out a burst of laughter. "Me? Oh, you have no idea what I've been doing for the last eight years. I'm the least likely person anyone is going to offer the rule to. It's got to be you, or I suppose Susanna."

Her littlest sister—all Mandy's memories were of an awkward ten-year-old with two left feet. "But she's just a baby."

Her sister raised a brow. "She's eighteen, but she's a far better choice than me."

They caught up a little more, then Mandy gave her sister a kiss on the cheek and brought the conversation back to Danielle's demand. "I can't give you an answer right now, I need to talk to people. Talk to...friends...and find out what they suggest."

Danielle hesitated. "Is that big bear one of the *friends*?"

Mandy saw no reason to lie. "Yes."

Her sister nodded slowly. "Okay. And by the way, I do trust you to do the right thing. We've been away from each other for a long time, but I always knew you were doing what you could for the family." She made a face. "Marrying Todd, then staying away and all."

It had been the only choice she could make, no matter how big a sacrifice. "If I hadn't cut myself off from the family, Todd would have taken over the island and become a vile dictator. It was the only way to save you all."

Danielle grimaced. "By sacrificing yourself."

Mandy shrugged. It was old, old news. It was the next decision she had to make that would change her life forever.

Her sister eyed her in confusion. "It might seem odd, but I do love you."

"In a 'locked up princess in a tower' kind of way?"

"In a 'I'm proud to be your sister' kind of way." Danielle stood determinedly, changing the topic as a mischievous smile curled her lips. "While you're deciding, are you planning on leaving me with that wolf?"

Mandy looked her little sister over with concern. "What did he do to you?"

Danielle's eyes widened. "Oh, no...nothing like that. Really, except..."

She glanced toward the door as it opened, and Cole marched back in, Justin at his side.

The big bear who'd been so much a part of her life the past week caught the wolf by the arm to keep him by the door. Cole's hungry gaze never once left Danielle, but Mandy's focus was on Justin.

On the sheer size of him, yet how he held himself in a protective way to make sure her wish for privacy was respected. How he looked her over rapidly to reassure himself that she wasn't hurt. Wasn't needing.

She *was* needing—time to think and to talk through what came next.

"Danielle, I'm going for a walk. Can you stay here for a while? Or do you need something to eat, or—"

"I'll stay with her." Cole was across the room and by their side in an instant.

Danielle rolled her eyes. "Sure, big guy. You can sit right here."

She dragged out one of the chairs and patted the seat before lowering herself into the one next to it.

Mandy wasn't sure what was going on, but she nodded. "I'll see you in a little while, okay? And then you can come back to our place, and we'll catch up a whole lot more."

"No prob, sis. Love ya." Danielle blew her a kiss then turned to the wolf. "You *are* a grumpy puppy, aren't you?"

Cole threw himself into the chair and growled at her, but this time it was a soft sound, as if he was trying to stop from laughing.

Justin took her arm and pulled her from the shop, back into the bright sunshine. "Come on. The fresh air will do you good."

Danielle waved her fingers then laid her hand on Cole's arm where it rested on the table between them. She looked as if she'd be fine, so Mandy glanced into Justin's face. "Fresh air sounds wonderful."

Justin wasn't sure at this point what his options were, and the ones that popped to mind first were bad and worse.

He knew what he wanted—Mandy.

But as she wandered at his side totally oblivious to their surroundings, he knew the answer wasn't as cut and dried as that.

Impulsively he caught her fingers in his. "Come on. I'm taking you for a ride."

She offered a soft laugh. "I'm in your capable hands."

Capable. *Ha.* A bear barely out of her teens had managed to elude him and his trackers. Tyler was going to laugh his ass off when he heard, and Caroline—

God, she'd never let him live this one down.

"I'm very impressed with your sister, by the way." He offered after popping Mandy in the Jeep and heading out of town. "Not many people can evade Cole, or the Takhini pack, for that matter."

"Danielle really did do a good job, didn't she? But

maybe she had a few tricks you weren't expecting," Mandy excused him

"Really? Are you trying to tell me the *ghost* in ghost bear means you can actually disappear?"

She smiled. "No, but I remember playing hide-and-go-seek with her before I moved away, and she was always a champion hider when motivated."

They sat in silence, the switchbacks of the road taking them higher and higher until they reached the point where they were looking over three different valleys. Mountains soared upward, the pale blue of the sky painted with delicate clouds.

He turned the Jeep into a lookout, and parked, joining Mandy at the railing where the entire valley lay at their feet.

"Danielle wants me to go back to the island."

"I heard."

She kept staring over the land. "She wants me to go back and take over the leadership—my Nana was in charge, and she's passed away."

He stifled his uncharitable thoughts about her grandmother, and focused on the idea Mandy might go away. Justin's heart fell to somewhere around his feet. "I'm sorry for your loss," he forced out as politely as possible.

Mandy offered him a sad smile. "Thank you, but I said goodbye to her years ago."

Justin laid a hand on her shoulder, needing to touch her. "So. What do you want to do? Do you want to rule?"

"You *knew*?"

He looked guilty for a moment. "Cole and I just google-fu'd the hell out of Kodiak Island using Danielle's and Susanna's names as an additional reference. Right around when you married Todd, the leadership was up for debate.

Your family, and one other. Yours turned out to have the most direct bloodline to the ghost bears who settled the island."

"We knew," she admitted. "Both the potential families knew our line was the one, but then the bear council put my name with Todd's for getting married, and everything changed."

Justin didn't understand. "I assume Todd pulled strings to get himself hitched to you. Why didn't the power-hungry bastard insist you stay on the island so he could take over?"

"Because he bribed the committee to marry me for my *title*. He had no idea I could potentially rule the entire island."

"Jeez, Mandy."

She shrugged. "Arranged marriages are the norm in bear society, you know that. If Todd had been a decent man, everything would have turned out differently, but at the start, we couldn't be sure."

Justin should've kept his mouth shut, but he simply couldn't. "I don't think much of your family for letting you make that sacrifice."

"It wasn't my sisters' fault." Mandy was quick to defend them. "But Nana..." She sighed before lifting sad eyes to meet his. "I've had moments I think ill of her, but I suppose she did what she thought was best for the people, and didn't question too hard when I chose to stay with Todd."

Mandy was too forgiving. Justin was ready to make heads fly on her behalf. He took a deep breath and shoved his anger aside so he could focus on being a rock for Mandy, here and now.

She was quiet for a long time before she finally spoke. "It's probably selfish and wrong, but I've given up so much of my life. I don't want to be all sacrificial again. I want to go explore the world, sleep in in the morning and read late. I want to get a dog—"

"Seriously? A *dog*?"

Her lips twitched. "Just making sure you're still listening."

He twisted her to face him fully. "I'm listening with everything in me. I don't think there's anything wrong in what you want."

"Is it selfish?"

"What makes it selfish? Just because you were born into a certain family that doesn't mean it's got to be you."

"If I don't...

"Then someone else will. Danielle's spent the last eight years on the island. Don't you think she might know a little better what's right for your people?

"That's blunt."

"Not that you wouldn't do an amazing job if you decided you wanted to, but, Mandy, that's why I asked the question. What do *you* want to do? And if it's sleeping late and reading books or traveling all over, you should do it."

"It's not that easy."

"It never is. But no matter what, you can take the time you need. You don't have to decide this moment."

Although he really wanted her to. He knew exactly what he wanted her to pick, but it was up to her. All he knew for certain was whichever road she took, he'd be right there beside her the entire time, no matter what.

From the moment she'd spotted her sister, all of the decisions she'd been putting off seemed to rise up like a tsunami wave, pulling her in a million directions.

Justin thought it was so simple. But Mandy had been gone long enough to barely know what Kodiak Island was like since she'd left.

She'd married Todd all those years earlier because it was how bear shifters did things. Finding out his true colours had meant she'd chosen to sacrifice her happiness to keep her family safe. She'd gone away, making sure that the mean bastard never knew what kind of money or power she could have accessed. Her silence had a huge cost, but it had been worth it.

Could she turn around after all that and deliberately walk back into a world where she wasn't in charge of her own life?

Then Justin was kissing her, lips brushing hers in a way that set her heart pounding and sucked the air from her lungs. Distracted her from the concerns swirling in her brain.

She let him tug her to the nearby lookout bench. "What was that for?" she asked.

"Because you looked as if you needed it. You looked as if you needed a reminder that I'm here, and that I promised to help. Offer still stands."

She stared back at the great big grizzly bear, with his massive arms, and huge torso, and his enormous heart that she swore she saw reflected in his mesmerizing eyes.

The daydreams she'd had about running around the world, and the dreams of exploring fabulous places, mixed with the dreams that she had about lying in bed on lazy mornings—they all were nothing until she imagined him there with her.

And that's when it hit her. She knew what she wanted, deep in her heart, and ultimately it wasn't a place, or a thing, or even a job description.

She looked into his big grey eyes. "Whatever I decide to do, what're *you* going to do?"

A soft laugh escaped him, and he shook his head slowly. "You're the one who's not listening. Wherever you go, and whatever you do, I'm going with you."

Mandy's heart fluttered. Hope rising. "And this is because?"

He smiled. "Because I'm a bear of many talents and few vices. The only real obsession I've got...is you."

He still wasn't saying it, and she wasn't sure she was brave enough to say it first.

Then, suddenly, she was.

"Justin, can I tell you something?"

One brow rose. "Of course."

She nodded decisively. "Whatever I do, I'm going to need help."

He waited patiently.

"You promised you'd help me with my list. What if the list suddenly had 'become leader of a small, wealthy island' on it?"

His eyes widened. "Is it likely to get added to your list? Is that what you really want?"

"I'm not sure," she admitted. "But I do know that I simply can't do anything on my list without the bear I love agreeing he's going to stay at my side. It's the one thing I can't—"

"Wait," he interrupted. "The bear you *love*?"

Mandy nodded. "Yup. Completely and thoroughly."

His smile started slowly then stretched into an all-out grin. "Well, of course it's completely and thoroughly. If you're going to do a thing, you've got to do it right."

Happiness snuck around the corners of the wall she'd

put up in case she *couldn't* have it all. "What about your job?"

Justin shrugged. "I work for Tyler because he's a friend and because it keeps me busy. If you need me, I'm all yours. You're way prettier to look at than him."

Mandy threw herself into his arms and kissed him hard before a sneaking thread of discontentment slipped through the bliss. "Wait—you didn't say it yet."

Justin caught her chin with his fingers and tipped her head back so he could kiss her easier. "Say what?"

She blew a raspberry. He blinked, a laugh rolling from him that started in his chest before rumbling up and sneaking out.

Mandy waited.

He dropped to one knee, tugging her hand to his lips so he could kiss her knuckles. "Lady Mandy, you have stolen something from me, so I now demand you care for it forever."

A soft warmth built inside. "What did I steal?"

He laid a hand on his chest. "My heart. The only reason I'm alive is this mysterious power that's taken its place. A magical power that makes my blood continue to pump, and my soul feel happiness."

She'd never dreamt he was such a poet, and the flowery language made her giggle. "I'm not sure if it's magical that I removed your heart, or shades of necromancy."

He chuckled then stage-whispered, "Go with it, my lady. Nadia's going to ask for all the details, and we may as well set the bar high."

"Like *wow* kisses for the wolves?"

"As long as it doesn't actually involve my lips near the pack, sure."

She sat on his knee and draped her arms around his shoulders. "I love you, Justin."

He leaned closer until their lips brushed. "I love you with everything in me."

That proclamation was as *wow* as it needed to be. It was *wow-to-the-wowwest* degree.

The drive back to Chicken seemed to take place in slow motion, his grip on her hand never loosening as she considered her decision, not coming to any quick solution.

Nadia was still leaning on the wall outside the shop waiting for them.

"You good?" she asked.

"Perfect," Mandy confessed. "Perfectly confused, but perfect."

Nadia grinned. "That's what I like to hear."

The room they entered was strangely quiet, and Mandy turned to Nadia in confusion. "Did Cole and Danielle go somewhere?"

Justin lifted his hand and pointed. "Damn."

Danielle was missing, but Cole was there, trussed up from head to foot, duct-taped to a chair with a piece of tape over his mouth.

Justin slid a knife through the mess holding him in place, but it was Nadia who reached out and ripped the covering from his mouth.

A wolfish roar of pain turned into a loud shout of anger as Cole took to his feet and whirled on them. "She's gone. She's been gone for half an hour, and now I'll have to track her down all over again."

"Good luck on that," Mandy uttered, ducking closer to Justin's side as the wolf offered her a nasty snarl.

"Back off," Justin warned. "It's hard to eat without

teeth, and it's even harder to track someone with a broken sniffer."

Cole snapped at Nadia. "Why didn't you stop her?"

"Because I only stop things from happening that shouldn't." She smirked at him.

He glared. "I did *not* want to be tied up."

Nadia raised a brow. "You sure, sweetheart? But wait—it's not me who needs to know all your kinky secrets. You'd better discuss that with Danielle when you catch her."

Loud growl. *Loud*.

"If you catch her."

He didn't bother responding, just turned his back and left at a full sprint, headed after his target again.

Mandy turned to Nadia. "We're going back to Whitehorse. I need to get in touch with my family, at least the part of it who isn't trying to evade a wolf, and figure out what comes next. Thank you for everything you did to make me comfortable during my time here."

Nadia gave her a hug. "I'm going to miss your happy smile. It was nice having a new girlfriend all of my own. You're welcome back anytime."

Mandy pressed closer to Justin's side as he tugged her against his body. "I think we'll be able to come visit."

"Of course we can," Justin agreed.

Saying farewell took a lot longer than she expected...but then again, maybe her expectations all needed to be revised. She'd made a lot of friends who all dropped by to say goodbye while she and Justin were packing, and with one thing and the other, it was a day later before they were ready to hit the road.

She stroked a hand over the dash of the camper. "Dale's going to want this back sometime."

"Yup," Justin agreed before flashing her a grin. "But for

now, it's ours, and we could check off an item from your list. You mind if we take a shortcut to get home? There's supposed to be a fabulous Aurora Borealis show over the next few nights..."

Mandy hesitated. "You don't think we should go straight home so I can decide?"

"Deciding will take some long walks and lazy mornings to think it all through. It's been eight years. You deserve a few more days."

"I suppose that would be okay. Where are the lights expected to be most visible?"

"Tombstone Park Campground on the Dempster highway."

Holy moly. "That's nowhere near Whitehorse."

"Nope."

She laughed. "That's probably as far north as we are now, and a lot more to the east. How is that a shortcut?"

"I don't know. But—" He pulled a piece of paper from his pocket and glanced at it. "There we go. This is what I meant to say."

She took the note from him, their fingers tangling together before she lifted the paper to the light to read out loud.

Make love under the Northern Lights.

Laughter bubbled up, and she was glad they were still motionless in the parking lot because that meant she could throw herself into his arms. "Funny, I don't remember that being on the list."

"Are you sure? It looks an awful lot like your handwriting—"

Whatever else he intended to say was lost. She was too busy kissing him. Holding him.

Claiming the bear who was her heart.

EPILOGUE

Dear Susanna,

I'm so pleased you've decided to accept the leadership of Kodiak Island. I know it's a big challenge, but all the people I spoke to when we visited a few weeks ago said you're the perfect person to take over for Nana. I can't tell you how proud it makes me to know you have the skills to take on the reins of the family tradition.

I know, it's kind of a bad pun. Reins, reigns. Let's blame it on the fact I'm a little giddy these days.

There's still been no trace of Danielle from our side. If you hear anything, let me know. I'm sure she's okay. She seemed very competent and determined, and everytime I ask Justin, he says to relax, as if he's got insider information he's not sharing.

Which means since I trust him—I'm relaxing. Hopefully we'll know more soon.

Justin and I will be dropping by again in the spring. We've decided to travel for a while—he's taking a leave of absence from his job and we're pretty much...well, just making a list and doing it. One day at a time.

I'm so happy.
Your loving big sister,
Mandy

JUSTIN HANDED the letter back to her when he finished reading it. "She's a great kid. And you're right—everyone we spoke to on the island is on board with her leading, even though she's young."

Mandy finished addressing the envelope. "Fortunately, being young is one thing that will slowly correct itself over time."

He laughed. "True enough."

Watching her move around the apartment—*their* apartment—was one more hit of pleasure in a long row of happiness.

She floated lazily, rearranging pillows and throw blankets. Hanging up tiny wooden reindeer ornaments. Her hands competent and steady, her eyes full of laughter and joy.

He'd been more than content to provide the labour as they furnished and decorated a two-bedroom place in Whitehorse. It might not be where they settled long term, but for now it was rapidly becoming home. Not only because of knickknacks and now the holiday decorations, but because of the pictures of them that kept showing up daily.

She'd done it again, he discovered. He slid his gaze off her to the frame she pulled from her shopping bag.

"Another one?" he asked with a laugh. "Let me see it."

Mandy all but bounced over to his side, holding out the photo eagerly. "This is my favourite so far."

He could see why. It was a group shot taken the

previous week at a barbecue get-together hosted by the other local bears in the area. Jim and Lillie Halcyon had opened their home and hearts to Mandy, especially Lillie.

The ladies were thick as thieves these days, and Justin was so glad. Having new girlfriends in her life was adding to the bloom in Mandy's cheeks.

The photographer had caught them in a moment of laughter, the posed assembly breaking apart into chaos, wearing wide grins and far-from-serious body positions. Evan and Amy were there, Jim and Lillie, Tyler and Caroline, and him and Mandy, all surrounded by more wolves than were safe to contain in one area.

The noise had been over the top, the jokes even worse—it had been like being back at the pack house, with one enormous difference.

He put the photo aside carefully so he could have both hands free to draw her into his arms. "It's almost my favourite," he told her.

Mandy tilted her head to the side, palms resting on his chest. "Which one do you like best?"

"The one we'll take tomorrow."

It took a moment as she considered his answer. "Where are we going tomorrow?"

"I have no idea, yet. But tomorrow, it'll be the picture we take the day after that..."

Her eyes lit with understanding. "We're never going to get around to taking your favourite!"

"We'll be taking pictures from now to forever, and I get to be in all of them with you." He kissed her. Slow and deep and needy until they were both breathless, then answered her. "You promised. I put it on the list."

Mandy blinked hard before her lips curled into a smile. She tugged him with her to the bedroom where in a moment of teasing he'd taken her original list and framed it, hanging it beside their bed.

She leaned in closer to check it out, and for the first time noticed the addition he'd made a few days ago. Her fingers tightened, and laughter burst from her, and then she was hugging him, and all was right in his world, because he knew she was going to work that list until it was done.

Good by him, since the new final item said:

spend my life with Justin, the bear who's madly in love with me

~

New York Times Bestselling Author Vivian Arend
brings you a series of light-hearted,
stand-alone novellas filled with shifters of all kinds—bears,
wolves, lynx. Whether they're fated mates or falling head-
over-paws, there's always a happily-ever-after.

~

Takhini Shifters
Copper King
Laird Wolf
A Lady's Heart
Wild Prince

~

ABOUT THE AUTHOR

New York Times and *USA Today* bestselling author Vivian Arend loves to share the products of her over-active imagination with her readers. She writes contemporary, western, and light-hearted paranormal romances. The stories are humorous yet emotional, usually with a large cast of family or friends, and a guaranteed happily-ever-after. Vivian lives in British Columbia, Canada, with her husband of many years—her inspiration for every hero and a willing companion for all sorts of adventures.

Find out more at www.vivianarend.com.